'You've force ~~loneliness,' K~~

'I'd convinced myself that I was meant to be on my own. And then you woke up!'

Jared could barely swallow the large lump in his throat. How badly he wanted to tell her the truth! But he was afraid it might be too soon. He realized he would have to court her, as he had the first time.

He skimmed his thumb over her soft lower lip. Small electrical charges quickened her pulse. 'What are you doing?' she asked.

'Nothing,' he claimed evasively as with slow, deliberate care he kissed her thoroughly. With a soft breathy moan she melted over him.

The kiss lasted only a few seconds and to all appearances was a playful exchange. But the two of them knew differently. They'd tasted liquid lightning.

'Where is this coming from?' Kate asked again. 'I mean, we never felt... It seems so soon. Too soon.'

'But surely not wrong,' he challenged.

'No.' She gazed down at her knotted fingers. 'Only too right.'

For Malle Vallik

May your heavenly
days be full of
chardonnay and shoes

———— 🍎 ————

**Leandra Logan is also the author of these
novels in *Temptation*®:**

HEAVEN-SENT HUSBAND

BY
LEANDRA LOGAN

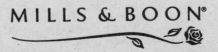

MILLS & BOON®

*MILLS & BOON and MILLS & BOON with the Rose Device
are registered trademarks of the publisher.
TEMPTATION is a registered trademark of
Harlequin Enterprises Limited, used under licence.*

*First published in Great Britain 1997
by Harlequin Mills & Boon Limited,
Eton House, 18-24 Paradise Road, Richmond, Surrey TW9 1SR*

© Mary Schultz 1996

ISBN 0 263 80452 6

21-9707

*Printed and bound in Great Britain by
Caledonian International Book Manufacturing Ltd, Glasgow*

1

SAM STONE WAS PLAYING with matches again.

His best friend and partner, Jared Reed, could smell it like the smoke of a distant fire.

An uneasy feeling had dogged Jared throughout the day as the self-employed private eyes had gone about their business. Their small, independent operation, Valley View Investigations, had successfully traced a teenage runaway that morning, then overseen the installation of a new security system for a downtown bank until late in the afternoon. All the while Jared had been aware of the edgy excitement beneath Sam's characteristic air of indifference, as though he had a hidden agenda.

Even now, as they rounded off the long day at a retirement party for police sergeant Walter Helser, Jared wondered. And worried . . .

The Lagoon Supper Club's party room was presently rocking with laughter as Walter stood at the podium, commenting on the sizzling roast he'd just endured at the hands of some of Denver's finest law enforcement people. The room was packed with well-wishers in a festive mood for the popular desk sergeant's send-off.

It was important that Jared try to keep in the spirit of things, especially for his wife Kate's sake. But the tension between him and Sam had not gone unnoticed by the raven-haired beauty seated between them, and she had been slanting them both suspicious looks.

Out of consideration, Jared had told her nothing of his apprehension. Walter and his wife, Martha, were like family to Kate and she was worrying about Walter, forced to retire after forty years of being in the hub of things at Denver's downtown Metro Station, was going to fare. Jared, who'd relied on Walter's inside information and professional advice for years and knew him to be indestructible, tried to convince her she was overreacting. His efforts were fruitless.

Kate was just too good to people. Too loving, too caring, too protective.

He thanked heaven every day that he was one of the people she gave entirely too much of herself to. Wished he could whisk her home this very second for the intimate chat she'd wanted.

But he'd have to deal with Sam first. The party was breaking up and his buddy appeared on the point of combustion. A new nervous tick marred his sharp, handsome features and his clumsy motor skills hinted at drunkenness.

"I believe I'll go say good-night to Walter and Martha," Kate said suddenly. She rose from her chair, smoothed her sapphire silk dress over her long, trim form, and patted her long tide of glossy black hair, all with an air of expectation. "Neat idea, Jared?"

Jared gazed up at her with absent fondness. "Sure, honey."

Kate's eyes crinkled and her mouth opened, but if she was going to say something, she reconsidered.

Sam watched her sashay away with an appreciative eye. "I think she wanted you to follow, soldier."

Jared's golden brows arched with interest. "You sound like you're trying to get rid of me."

Baring his square white teeth, Sam planted his palms on the table and rose with effort. "I am."

Jared affected a jolly tone. "Hey, what's your hurry?"

Sam tugged his black leather jacket from the back of his chair, and eased it on rather awkwardly. "Sleepy."

Suspicion tightened Jared's chest. He stood, fighting to keep up a relaxed social front. "Oh, c'mon, this doesn't sound like you. Even in junior high you were good till midnight."

Sam stared down at his wiry blond friend, his green eyes flashing with annoyance. "Go be with your wife, Jare."

"See what I mean?" Jared said incredulously. "You never say that, either!"

With a frustrated growl Sam brushed by him, then wove through the tangle of small linen-covered tables like a black whipcord.

Jared took a surreptitious inventory of the dining room, hoping that no one, Walter in particular, had witnessed Sam's rude exit. The old duffer certainly didn't deserve this kind of snub. Luckily, Walter was buried five rows deep in people who wanted to say goodbye and shake his hand. Satisfied that he wouldn't be missed, either, Jared went in pursuit of his pal.

Sam was just outside the entrance, leaning against a huge potted tree, gulping cool night air. Jared skidded to a stop beside him. They stared each other down for a long, belligerent moment.

"Leave me alone." Sam ground out the words in an angry rush, betraying a noticeable slur in his speech.

"You been hitting the booze?" Jared asked in amazement. "Is that what you've been hiding from me all day?"

"Thah's stupit." Sam tipped his head back against the tree trunk, his guard slipping. "You know better."

"I know you sound bad and look even worse. I know I have a funny feeling."

Sam hissed like a snake, "I juss hate it when you get a funny feeling. Juss hate it!"

Jared grabbed a handful of soft Italian leather as Sam launched himself toward the parking lot. They twisted and tussled beside the curb like overgrown kids.

"Hey! Stop it! Before somebody sees you." Kate Reed marched out from under the maroon awning over the entrance in a cyclone clatter of high heels.

"He's trying to ditch me," Jared blurted incredulously.

"Let him," she snapped. "By all means!"

Sam stopped struggling and leered at Kate. "Hmm, she's on my side for once. Now *I* got a funny feeling."

Kate gave him the look she used on her unruly seventh grade students. He certainly knew better than to try his dangerous wolf act on her, didn't he? She'd been immune to his charms for nearly a decade!

"He isn't himself, Kate," Jared attempted to explain. "It has to be the beers, I guess."

Her eyes widened. "It takes more than a couple of drinks to put him in a lampshade condition."

"I never wear a lampshade on my head," Sam objected huffily. "A garter maybe . . ."

"Oh, yes," Kate returned smoothly. "Sweet memories of my own wedding, my own garter."

"It had those pistols."

She gasped in affront. "It did not!"

Jared approached his wife with a beseeching look. "Kate, honey, please keep your sense of humor. You can see that he's not quite with it."

"I think he's playing games with both of us," she declared, folding her arms across her chest.

Sam used the diversion to his advantage, escaping across the blacktop like a light-headed black panther not quite up to the prowl. Jared caught up with him just as he reached his cherry-colored Camaro. Sam whirled sharply, clutching his temples as a fresh wave of dizziness overtook him.

"Steady, Sam."

Sam leaned against his car's back fender. "I'm . . . a little tired."

The club's double doors flung open behind them, spilling out a flood of bodies and noise.

Jared and Kate exchanged a significant look and closed ranks on Sam, each taking an elbow. They would keep this situation between themselves.

"What's this?" Sam griped, trying to wrench free.

Jared gave him a nudge. "It's taken us twelve years to build Valley View into a top-notch agency, respected by the department, and you're not going to flush it down the can by acting like a buffoon."

As they bid good-night to passersby, Kate fingered Sam's supple leather sleeve, thinking it would keep them in groceries for a month. If only he would grow up, branch out on a meaningful course of his own. He'd been in the same groove since childhood, preferring the schoolboy closeness with Jared to any adult-size emotional challenges. All in all, he seemed a hopeless case to her.

"Jared, I want to go home," she pressed, openly troubled. "Bonny's baby-sitter is only fourteen and it's close to midnight."

Jared's expression softened as he thought of their six-year-old daughter, the mirror image of him with a head of blond curls, huge blue eyes and round, dimpled cheeks. He shared Kate's worry. Bonny was getting over an ear infection and was running a mild fever. He side-stepped Sam and tugged his wife to his length. Both stood at about five foot eight, which made intimate conversations easy.

"You're right, of course," he crooned, rubbing her nose with his.

"And you know I wanted to talk to you," she whispered. "It's very important."

His hands skimmed the silky surface of her back, the tips of his fingers tingling. "I know. Can't wait . . ."

"Then let's sort out Sam and—"

"Well, if it isn't The Three Musketeers!" Walter's familiar voice boomed nearby.

Jared cautioned Sam to silence, then turned with Kate to greet the Helsers. The tall, large-boned pair was laden with the gag gifts presented to Walter at the dinner—a jumble of mugs, T-shirts and gadgets.

"Have a nice time?" Kate asked affectionately. Her relationship with the Helsers dated back to when Martha had been her eighth grade English teacher. The product of a dysfunctional family, Kate had been in desperate search of a role model. Martha had taken her under her wing, and had introduced her to the fulfilling career of teaching. They'd worked alongside each other at a local school until Martha's retirement two years ago.

"We had a wonderful time," Martha enthused, nearly losing a neon cap from her bundle. "Hope Bonny's all right."

"She's tucked in bed," Kate reported, "waiting to hear all about Walter's loot."

Walter's bristle brows rose like twin toothbrushes. "We'll stop by tomorrow for some show and tell. It's Saturday, so I'll be free."

"You'll be free everyday from now on, dear," Martha teased.

Walter gulped. "It'll take some getting used to, all the spare time."

Everyone chuckled. Martha shifted her parcels again and tipped her head in the direction of their vehicles, parked side by side in the rear of the lot. "If you two are leaving, help us carry this stuff!"

Jared declined with a shake of his head, feeling a little like a heel. "We have some business to settle." The Helsers seemed genuinely disappointed, so he added, "We'll fire up the barbecue tomorrow, though. Keep this party going with Bonny's help."

Once the elder pair moved on, Jared whirled back on Sam angrily. "I've had it. What gives?"

Sam sagged against the Camaro's trunk with droopy lids. "Lemme alone. Never ask you for another thing. Promise."

"Never ask me—" Jared laughed in disbelief. "See what I mean, Kate? Sam's off the deep end! I'd better run him home in his car."

Kate's thick black lashes swept over disappointed eyes. "What about a taxi?"

Jared considered it carefully. "The Camaro's too flashy to leave in this part of town all night. It just might disappear before sunrise."

"Maybe Walter—" She stopped in mid-sentence as the Helser's old silver Buick rumbled to life and began to roll away. "That was quick. But I suppose they're exhausted."

He smiled tentatively at his wife. "Do you mind, going on ahead with the van?"

She sighed in surrender, digging into her evening bag for her key ring. "All right."

"Thanks." Jared cupped her face and covered her mouth with his hungrily for a brief taste. He ached to follow her like a frisky puppy. But he always felt like that to some degree. Two years of courting, seven years of marriage, and his wife still seemed the most desirable woman in the world to him. "I'll hurry," he whispered. "Spill him at his apartment and be home before you know it." He gave her bottom a gentle pat. "Now, shoo, so I can watch you get off safely."

Both men watched her cross the lot, her long slender body fluid beneath her silky dress, her black hair waving like a banner in the breeze. Jared's sigh was weighted with guilt and regret when he eventually reached into Sam's jacket pocket for his car keys, and poured his pal into the passenger seat.

Jared's mouth crooked boyishly as he slipped into the snug driver's seat and inched closer to the wheel. Handling this machine was one small consolation for playing guardian. Jared didn't regret buying Kate's van or his own gray four door Lumina; it was all part of the family package, along with the ranch-style house in the suburbs. But he wondered what it would be like to walk in Sam's shoes, to be the tall, dark and handsome type so irresistible to the female population.

The fleeting thought faded into oblivion where it belonged as Jared caught a glimpse of his reflection in the rearview mirror. His own roundish face and crimped golden hair had served him well enough. According to Kate, his clear blue eyes were the dreamiest imaginable. Small mirrors reflecting strength and integrity.

So how'd he end up with Sam on this lovely May night, when the most beautiful girl in the world wanted him all to herself?

"We gotta get you a woman," Jared muttered, bringing the engine rumbling to life. "One stable, loyal dupe, so stuck on you that she'd find this kind of behavior cute."

Sam, rubbing his face with trembling hands, struggled with his speech. "Don't know what's wrong with me."

Jared made a disgusted sound as he swung out of the lot. "Sleep it off and we'll talk about it in the morning."

"It'll be too late then!"

"What will?"

"Business meeting, Jare. All set up. I can't miss it."

Was Sam playing games, as Kate suspected? Jared gave the situation some thought as they cruised down Alameda Avenue. Deals did go down late sometimes. Sam usually worked the night shift alone, when he made contact with Denver's seedier side for the agency. "Why didn't you say something about this hours ago?"

"Made a promise. No you, no cops."

That sometimes happened, too, Jared reluctantly conceded, slowing for an amber light. His link to the Helsers and straight-shooter methods were well-known facts that made some shadier types nervous. Sam was viewed as more of an enigma, known to cut legal and ethical corners when necessary.

"Anybody else would run this red," Sam complained, craning his neck with exaggeration as he checked out the empty intersection.

"You'd run it, Sam," Jared returned evenly. "That isn't everybody." He took his partner's griping with practiced patience. He often speculated that if they hadn't been boyhood friends back in Boulder, they probably wouldn't have clicked as adults. But a mutual caring had evolved between them, like mismatched brothers who couldn't live with or without each other.

"You juss don't understand," Sam bit out.

"Only because you refuse to tell me anything!" Jared retorted. "Sorry, but no deal is worth this kind of runaround. It's home for both of us."

"Okay, it's the Carson Collection," Sam begrudgingly admitted.

That got Jared's attention. He sat in the intersection on the green light until the driver in the sedan behind him tapped his horn. "You're joking! Aren't you?"

"About money?" Sam sat back with a satisfied smirk as Jared regarded him with new interest. "Somebody wants to return it to the insurance company through me," he explained, enunciating carefully, "for a measly ten percent of our finder's fee."

Jared's excitement faded to wariness of the bargain basement offer. The famed jewelry collection had been stolen from the Colorado State museum a couple of months ago. Crafted for Willard X. Carson, one of Golden's most prosperous gold miners a century ago, the pieces were eventually willed to the state. Mutual Trust Insurance held the policies for all the museum's general contents and had engaged Valley View to dig into the matter. Hungry for the two hundred thousand dollar finder's fee, Jared and Sam had given it their best shot. Unfortunately, they'd made little progress, and were eventually forced to focus on their more routine cases that brought in sure, flat fees.

"This seems too good to be true," Jared objected. "Who'd give up two million dollars in jewelry for a measly twenty thousand?"

Sam was affronted by the question. "An amateur who couldn't fence that gaudy stuff on the street. Just as we hoped!"

Jared remained unconvinced. "Why not deal with the insurance company directly for the whole reward? They're desperate to make a deal—with anybody."

Sam's speech was thick, but he struggled to be concise. "The insurance company would call the cops 'cause there's a murder charge, with that guard dying of a heart attack. I'm a much smaller risk, a good go-between."

"Because you'd make the deal and not worry about your moral obligation concerning the guard," Jared interpreted with a fair amount of disgust.

"Aw, nobody laid a hand on him."

"It's true, the circumstances of the robbery most likely gave the old guard's heart a fatal jolt. But the letter of the law is clear on the subject. When somebody dies during the course of a crime, it's murder pure and simple."

Sam slapped his head back against the seat. "See why nobody calls you first?"

Jared chuckled. "How do you know this is even on the level? Could be a crackpot on the streets who wants to yank you around a little."

Sam gestured to a closed service station and popped open the glove compartment. "Pull in there."

Jared obeyed, braking under a fluorescent light. To his amazement, Sam produced a ring, with a large ruby set on high golden prongs.

"Satisfied?"

Jared nodded mutely, recognizing it from the museum photos back in the office case file. "Where did it come from?"

Sam smirked, like a fisherman reeling in a prize trout. "Came by messenger yesterday, after I agreed to the deal by phone."

"Which messenger service? One we know?"

"Mrs. Ginty, my neighbor across the hall with the parakeets, took the package. Just remembers that it was a young man with a cap pulled down over his fore-head."

"Someone trying to avoid direct contact with you, maybe."

"Or somebody just trying to avoid our office, you and our nosy Eve."

Jared couldn't deny that he and their pert reception-ist probably would've grilled the messenger.

"There was a map, too." Sam reached over to the driver's side visor and pulled loose a folded sheet of paper.

Jared opened the map under the light, noting that it was hand-drawn. A fingerprint check and other anal-yses should be done, but all that would have to wait. "Creekside Tavern, eh? Never heard of it."

"It's one of those touristy places just out of the Estes. I called to make sure it was real."

Jared took a closer look at the map. "Estes Park? You were planning to drive all the way up there?"

"Still am. And I'm late."

"Oh, Sam, it's two hours in the best conditions."

"I know that!"

Jared glanced toward the glove compartment again and spied a white envelope. "I suppose you have the twenty grand payoff in there."

Sam nodded his dark head with confidence. "Yep. Cleaned out most of my account."

Jared moaned. "This is so risky."

"Bet you and Kate could use your share of the re-ward," Sam tempted softly. "A cool hundred grand would make you look like a big shot."

"Yeah, especially now," Jared blurted, real pleasure in his voice for the first time. "I think that I'm going to be a daddy again. Kate has some kind of big news for me, and a second baby is the only thing that makes sense. The due date would be timely, too," he went on. "Close to the end of the next school year, when they could ease in a substitute teacher for her class. With the whole summer as bonus leave."

"Another Bonny would be nice." Sam adored the child who called him uncle.

"A boy would be great, too," Jared said pensively.

Sam scratched his square chin. "Don't know if I can charm a boy..."

"Let's get back to business."

"I'm feeling better now."

Jared had to admit that Sam's speech was clearing up, but he noted that his hands, planted on the dashboard, still trembled. "You're still in no condition to drive, especially not on mountainous roads."

"So drive me, Jare."

Should he? Jared was on edge trying to decide. He'd promised Kate he'd be back. But wouldn't she understand about the detour? She knew how hard they'd worked to track down the collection. If there was a chance of wrapping up the case with a few more hours' work, wasn't it worth a try? "If I take you," he began slowly, "I'm in all the way, at your side. I also want to carry the ring and the agency gun."

Sam frowned, but agreed.

"Also, if an arrest is possible, I intend to make good on it."

"Can I at least carry my own money?" Sam asked caustically.

"Sure. It's your show, remember?" Jared ignored his partner's sarcastic thank yous and picked up Sam's cellular phone to contact Kate on her way home. He got no answer. "Our telephone must be in the Lumina. I'd better call the sitter at the house."

He did his best to explain things to the girl, but realized most of his enthusiasm would be lost in the translation. Ah, but the money would make up for it in the end. Kate would be so busy spending it on Bonny and the new nursery that she wouldn't have time to be annoyed with him!

2

THE CREEKSIDE TAVERN proved to be a place common to the area, a log cabin structure nestled in the trees, open 'round the clock with homemade food, strong black coffee, two brands of beer and red house wine.

It was close to two-thirty when Jared and Sam sauntered in. With the possible exception of the contact, no one would suspect that the short, fair-haired man was packing a pistol under his tweedy sport coat or that the taller dark one had twenty grand tucked away in the lining of his leather jacket.

Customers were sparse at the late hour. A few male truckers were playing poker in a front booth, and some women in tight clothes and heavy makeup sat at the lunch counter sipping draft beer. All of them had miles on them in one form or another.

Jared and Sam chose a square table in the back with a clear view of the whole place. They exchanged frowns of disappointment as they scraped back the chairs and sat down. Nobody seemed interested in them.

"This doesn't look promising," Sam muttered, squinting at a skinny brunette on one of the worn stools, who was recrossing her legs ever so slowly to give him a sample of her charms.

Jared saw a lot more of the short-skirted contortion-ist than he'd like. "Can't you shut off your charisma somehow?" he asked in a disgusted whisper.

"I didn't do anything!"

"Sam, you winked."

"I blinked," he insisted. "Have something in my eye."

"Wink again and she'll come over," Jared predicted with sour certainty.

"So I won't blink again. Satisfied?"

Jared was satisfied that Sam's head was clearing. He was far sharper than he'd been.

"Not that anything matters anymore," Sam grum-bled. "We're late. Too late."

Jared's mouth compressed as he held his temper. "We got here as fast as we could."

Sam jabbed a finger in his face. "No, we got here as fast as *you* could."

"A little faith, a little patience, won't kill you," Jared chided.

The only server in the place was a forty-something male built like a refrigerator, with a flattop haircut and white uniform stained with ketchup and grease. He was put out when they ordered only a pot of decaf, and left a carafe and cups with a thump. His mood didn't lighten when they requested a second round, either. After that, he stayed behind the counter, never giving them an-other glance.

"I've had enough," Sam eventually declared about four o'clock, tossing some bills on the table to cover their check. The only moves they'd made all night were to the rest room, one at a time, so as not to miss anything. Unfortunately, there'd been nothing to miss: no interested contact, no treasure trove of jewels.

Jared had been ready to leave for quite some time, but didn't want Sam to accuse him of being too hasty. So he'd sat, wishing he was at home, waiting for Sam to lead the way.

Jared didn't waste any more time however; he charged out the door and across the gravel parking lot at a brisk, crunching clip. If they got moving, he'd be home to greet his girls at the breakfast table. "I may as well drive back," he said, jingling the keys. "You still look sort of ragged at the edges."

Sam yawned as he eased into the passenger side of the Camaro. "Don't know what's gotten into me. Feel like I could sleep forever."

"Me, too. Let's roll down the windows to keep us alert." Jared couldn't help but take inventory of the interior, and was a little disappointed that there was no package or message anyplace.

They began their descent back to the arid plains and the city. The night sky was still fairly dark, and the dense forest lining the steep two lane road didn't offer any relief. The low-slung car whizzed along at a moderate pace, its highbeams illuminating the twisty path.

Despite the fresh air slapping their faces, Sam still managed to fall asleep in no time. Jared was frustrated. He wanted to talk about this setup, examine possible motives and courses of action.

As he weighed the situation to the tune of Sam's steady snore, his frustration was replaced by alarm. What was behind this good-for-nothing trip?

And who was behind them on the road? The head-lights of a full-size truck appeared intermittently in his rearview mirror, illuminating the interior of the car. Jared had vast experience with tailing techniques, having been both the hunter and the prey over the years. He tested the truck at various speeds. The other driver matched him mile for mile, keeping a measured distance. Was he playing it safe, or making it dangerous?

Jared's reliable private eye instincts sensed danger. This situation was a fine example of why he actually weighed the circumstances and options with care.

But like it or not, he'd leapt blindly this time. Fueled by greed and curiosity, he'd been every bit as impulsive and foolish as Sam.

He slanted Sam a worried look. Just as he'd thought, he wasn't even belted in. Bad news if the ride got wild. Which seemed likely, considering that the brakes weren't working as well as they had earlier on. Every time he depressed the pedal now, the car seemed more reluctant to respond.

"Sam!" He reached over to give his partner a nudge. Sam mumbled something about breakfast in bed and shifted his long legs in the cramped space.

"Stone!"

Jared downshifted with a grind of gears. That got Sam's attention. He sat up rigidly, his eyes snapping open.

"What the hell is that noise?"

Jared made a choking sound, his profile grim and pale. "I'm tr-trying to slow down."

"Use the brakes."

"They're out. All gone!" Jared's voice was a wail as he took the next curve with another grind of the gearshift. He was making all his turns as wide as possible in an effort to break their speed, hogging every inch of blacktop on both sides of the line. A car appeared on the incline suddenly, horn blaring. Tires squealed as the other car braked and Jared swerved to avoid impact.

Sam cursed as his head slammed into the door frame. "They can't be gone. This car is new." Sam's tone was so full of certainty that Jared couldn't help giving the pedal another frantic pump. Nothing.

"I think we're being followed, too," Jared reported tersely, his eyes never leaving the windshield now.

Sam twisted around to study the rear. The other vehicle was just rolling out from behind a rock formation. "Looks like an extended pickup."

"And roars like something much bigger." Jared's fingers curled around the steering wheel even tighter. "Better buckle up."

"Seat belt's jammed," Sam growled, trying to yank it free. "Been meaning to fix it."

"And the brakes?"

"They were fine, I tell you. Somebody must've messed with them back there!"

Jared knew in his jackhammering heart that Sam was probably right. But he was in no position to analyze what was happening as he guided them down, down the snaky line of blacktop. At some points the road was cut into the mountainside, at others it was lined with huge cedar trees. Capped by a charcoal sky, it was often like whizzing through an underground tunnel. For the first time ever, Sam was struck speechless. Only wheezing sounds came from the passenger side of the car every time Jared drove the Camaro onto the gravel shoulders, perilously close to walls of stone and tree, in an effort to shave their speed. They were doing seventy into the turns.

Only minutes had passed as they hurtled down the mountain road, but it seemed longer because every second was magnified by their terror, their fear of almost certain death.

"Take the next clearing!" Sam shouted. "Dive into the trees."

It would be a crap shoot, Jared knew. Many of the clearings dropped off into steep hillsides. It was impossible to recognize a safe spot at the rate they were traveling.

"Dive! Jerk the wheel. Spin around."

Jared nodded grimly. It had to be done. And there was a small stretch of straight road ahead with possibilities. With a steady grip on the wheel, he proceeded with purpose.

Then came the familiar glint in the rearview mirror. The truck was bearing down on them, matching their perilous speed. Soon the vehicles were fender to bumper, the truck's high beams illuminating the Camaro's interior like a shadow box. Jared's and Sam's eyes met for a split second, casting horrified silhouettes on the back window.

Jared steered into the clearing. A stand of solid cedar trees curtained the ravine from view, making it impossible to calculate the size of the clearing. But the sound of the rushing river echoing up the rocks was frighteningly close.

There was a hope that the trucker's motives had been misjudged by two paranoid private eyes. But all was lost when the truck moved up beside them as they careened into the clearing, cutting off any escape back onto the road, boxing them into a corridor between the truck and trees.

Jared's foot automatically hit the brake pedal over and over again as they whizzed toward the ravine's guardrail with their deadly escort. Images of Kate and Bonny filled his mind suddenly; the last wish granted a dying man.

Terrified sounds ripped from their throats as the ailing, dented Camaro crashed through the rail and shot like a rocket down the hillside. It hit a cluster of spruce strong enough to break their speed and pop the doors open. Unbelted, Sam bounced free and tumbled into the brush. Jared, knocked unconscious by the impact with the trees, didn't have the chance to unbuckle for the same kind of escape. He took the ride all the way down to the deep dark water's edge below.

JARED AWOKE in a hushed pocket of blue and white light. The oppressive darkness and piercing headlights of the accident still filled his mind, but not the terror. Never before had he felt so safe. Blessedly, gloriously safe.

Unbelievably safe.

Panic rose as he mentally backtracked through the events of the accident, scanning for memories of a rescue. Nothing materialized.

But that alone didn't mean anything. Drugs would explain this floaty state. Of course! Injury was inescapable. He was probably flat on his back in a hospital room, anesthetized for his own comfort.

It was a blessing he couldn't see or feel right now. The pain would probably kill him.

"Help!" With a burst of courage he cried out into the vast nothingness. "Can anyone hear me?"

"Of course, Jared," a gentle voice replied.

Jared stared into the soft light but could see nothing. "Am I drugged?" he asked nervously. "Drugged and hallucinating?"

"No, it's all very real."

"The crash," he persisted. "What happened? Why don't I remember?"

"You were knocked unconscious. It was over quickly, and relatively painlessly. A merciful end."

End to what? The accident? Or more? "Am I all right?"

"Yes, certainly."

"Alive and well?" It took all his courage to press the issue and wait for the answer.

"The crash was fatal, Jared. You died of a broken neck."

The news sent his thoughts spinning in a circle going nowhere. Jared was a problem solver, an optimist, a goal setter. For the first time ever he couldn't see beyond the moment; the awful reality set before him with no escape, no second chance. It just wasn't right! It wasn't fair! "Where am I now, this minute?" he eventually asked numbly. "Heaven?"

"Not technically. Not yet."

"I don't understand."

"You are on the other side of heaven, or the other side of earth, if you prefer. You are drifting between the two planes of existence, in a phase of adjustment."

"But I don't want to adjust! There has to be a mistake."

"The very reason for your holding pattern, Jared. You don't wish to be here and we weren't expecting you."

"Oh." Suddenly he thought of Sam and asked about him.

No sooner did he ask than he was infused with a wealth of information and vivid images. Sam was in surgery at Denver Community Hospital. A surgical team was working to repair his punctured lung. His dynamic body was still, pale and fragile on the table. "Is he going to make it?"

"Conceivably, he could," the voice replied mildly. "The team is sure he will. It's not his destiny, however, to survive."

"Are you saying our destinies were scrambled somehow?"

"Yes, in a way. The driver of the Camaro was to be broken beyond repair. And you put yourself behind the wheel. Understand?"

Jared was stunned. "Sam was supposed to be driving? I was supposed to be the passenger?"

"Jared, Jared, you weren't even supposed to be along for the ride."

Anger flooded him. "Why didn't you stop me, then?"

"Signals were sent, Jared. Strong ones. You, unfortunately, misinterpreted them."

"But I tried to do right. Sensed trouble and acted accordingly."

"We know. And to your credit, you've used your intuitive gift wisely over the years. But this time the wires got crossed and you answered the wrong SOS. Man's freedom of choice sometimes causes these mix-ups to happen."

"Kate needed me more then?" he wondered dubiously.

"In this instance, yes."

"But she agreed with my decision," he argued defensively.

"She surrendered to your wishes. There is a difference."

"But how could I have given Sam his freedom in his condition?" he challenged.

"Kate gave you the answer herself."

"The taxi," he recalled dully. "But I was afraid Sam would loop around the block and pick up his car just the same."

"His free choice, his fated choice. To drive into the foothills alone, to die alone."

"I was only trying to do the right thing," Jared insisted in anguish.

"It was a tough call. But you made a series of mistakes with Sam. He took advantage of you at every turn. Kate tried to tell you, but every time your wife needed you and Sam demanded your attention, as well, she was forced to compromise."

"But no one else truly cared about Sam," he argued. "Growing up in a boys' home run by the county, he had nobody but me."

"Your family's good will was his chance to get a decent foundation. Unfortunately, he didn't follow the signposts set along the way. He shunned opportunities to grow and mature, took the easy way out every time."

"No, he just couldn't seem to get his act together."

"Which behooved us to transfer him to another life for another chance. He was stumbling along a dead-end path and his spirit is too strong to waste."

"So, he'll be okay."

"Jared, it's time to stop working your caretaker's soul so hard. It's time to rest."

"But I can't rest. Not with a wife and child relying on me! I need a second chance of my own."

"But your body was destroyed."

"A facsimile would do," Jared proposed anxiously. "Surely you could whip something up."

"Certainly. But you were properly buried, so all you'd manage to do is scare your loved ones to their own deaths."

"Oh. See your point."

"You are scheduled to return eventually. From scratch, as an infant, in the next millennium."

"That will be too late. Bonny will be a teenager by then. I have to get back now. Kate's waiting. Waiting up for me." His voice broke under the strain.

"Time is relative here. Observe Sam once more. He is now lying comatose in a private room, three and a half weeks since the accident. Ah, such a waste of a good human vessel. In any case, he'll be leaving it behind very soon."

Jared surveyed the cheery room full of stuffed animals and balloons, gifts from Sam's airhead girlfriends. How amazing that nearly a whole month had passed during the brief conversation. "Why delay his death?" Jared wondered aloud suddenly. "Unless . . . are you doing it for me because I've put up such a stink? Preserving Sam's body as an alternative home for my spirit?"

"The phrase 'putting up a stink,' doesn't do service to your fortitude. But you are correct about the option. We, too, would like you back on earth to fulfill your destiny. But this change in body is one you should consider carefully."

"I don't have to!" he rejoiced. "It'll put me back, right where I belong. Within reach of my girls."

"The adjustment is bound to be complex and difficult. To the world, you'll be Sam Stone."

"True, but I'll be at the right place at the right time."

"There are many complications in the deal. Some dangerous."

Jared gave the point due consideration. Someone wanted Sam dead. Badly. But the pain of losing Kate far outweighed any imaginable peril.

That truth realized, Jared was prepared and determined, infused with a dose of his old optimism. He had a plan again, hope again, a chance again.

"There are no guarantees, Jared," the voice broke in to caution. "This fresh start is a wild card in the deck. You'll be charting a new and unexpected path, reshaping your slice of fate with your wits and courage."

"I'm determined to try."

"Goodbye for now, then. And good luck."

3

"DR. GLENBROOK HERE, Mrs. Reed. I hate to disturb you on this beautiful Saturday afternoon, but Sam Stone's been asking for you again."

Kate leaned against the kitchen counter, the cordless phone in her hand, and a gasp of surprise escaped her lips before she could pinch them shut. She didn't want to appear rude, but Sam's new interest in her was downright unbelievable as well as disturbing. It was three months since the accident, and the shock of her husband's tragic death had begun to subside. To have to cope with Sam's persistent requests to see her seemed unfair.

She had to admit, though, it was all brand new to Sam. He'd only been awake for two weeks and was just beginning to deal with the reality of life without Jared. Apparently he'd been asking for her since his eyes had popped open during a sponge bath. He'd taken one look at the startled nurse's aid and had mistaken her for Kate.

She'd never quite understood what happened next. But apparently the aid had dropped ten pounds since and was frequently found singing in the stockroom. It seemed even an incapacitated Sam could entertain and delight.

"It's time for his discharge, you see," Dr. Glenbrook continued on a kindly note. "His car was destroyed in the accident as you know, leaving him with no way to get home."

"I can't imagine why he's so interested in me," she sputtered, nervously fingering the jet black tresses curving her collarbone. She never should've gotten her hair cut. It was way too hard to twist it around her fingers now.

"Perhaps you represent a level of comfort to him, Mrs. Reed. The homefires angle."

"Sam doesn't value those things!" Her tone was without animosity, for she'd long ago accepted Sam for what he was: a charming Romeo determined not to give any part of himself away to anyone.

"He may seem careless on the surface. But it's a known fact that when we're feeling frightened and alone, we're unconsciously drawn to what's real and secure."

"Yes, I suppose so." Kate swallowed hard. Realism and security were subjects that choked her up quickly these days. She stared through the billowing white chiffon fringing the back window, determined not to cry again. It had been weeks since the funeral, but only minutes since her daughter Bonny had asked about her daddy's return. At the time of his death, Jared had been in the process of building Bonny a life-size playhouse in the rear of the yard between two of their larger maple trees. The structure stood half finished and Bonny was anxious for its completion. The curly topped child was back there now, carrying on a conversation with some robins fluttering around a nest in the taller tree.

Kate couldn't make out what she was saying from this distance, but the sound of her little voice carried on the breeze with a songbird sweetness of its own.

"But doctor," she continued, "Sam is a very popular guy. You saw for yourself the company he attracted during his hospital stay."

Dr. Glenbrook grunted in understanding. "Lovely young creatures with squeaky voices and limited clothing budgets."

Underdressed dumbbells, Kate silently translated in wholehearted agreement.

"It's true they hung around while he was under," Glenbrook went on. "But he's refused to speak to a single one since he awoke. I've been forced to deal with them myself!"

"With your busy schedule?" Kate was surprised. "That's very nice of you, doctor."

"Well, after all Sam's been through, I must admit I've taken a protective interest in him. Throughout this whole ordeal his vital signs fluctuated wildly between life and death, like an old generator fighting for salvation. You also fretted over him during the darkest days," he reminded her gently.

"He was unconscious then. Easy to handle."

"Please help him over one more hurdle—get him settled in his apartment. Even if it's just in the interest of science. You see, I wouldn't want Sam to backslide when I'm so close to pinpointing the source of his sexual magnetism. I want to put it in a pill and sell it!"

His humor was infectious. Kate found herself laughing out loud. "All right, I'll come. It will take some time, though. I have to find a sitter for Bonny."

He drew a hesitant breath. "Would you mind bringing your daughter along?"

She blinked in perplexity, gripping the receiver tighter. "Why?"

"Sam specifically asked that you do. Please."

"Are you sure we're dealing with the same Sam?"

"Trauma can do strange things to people. You may be in for some surprises."

The physician hung up the telephone at the fourth floor nurse's station and moved down the corridor to Sam Stone's room. He pushed the door open to find Sam sitting up in bed, studying his face in a small gold-framed mirror presented to him by the infatuated nurses. Never in his long career as a surgeon had Thomas Glenbrook seen anyone so intrigued by his own face—including female patients freshly healed from plastic surgery!

"Well, Sam, it looks like your getaway car will be pulling up soon."

"Kate's coming, doc?" Jared demanded earnestly over the mirror. "Now? Right now?"

Glenbrook nodded his silver head. "Yes, as fast as she can manage."

"Thank God!" Jared threw his hands up in the air, wincing over the pain the sudden movement caused his rib cage.

The doctor moved to his bedside, and extracted a penlight from the pocket of his white lab coat. "Head feeling clear as a bell?"

"Absolutely," Jared insisted.

Dr. Glenbrook clicked on the light and shone it in one eye, then the other. "Pupils look fine. Shall we go through our routine once more for old times' sake?"

"Knock yourself out," Jared invited with forced joviality. He was still uncomfortable with some of the doctor's questions and hated this routine.

"What's the month?"

"August."

"Your birthday?"

Jared paused, reviewing Sam's statistics. "December first."

"Your address?"

"Uh, 272 Windham Road, Apartment 2A."

The doctor winced and hesitated. "I wish you were a little quicker with these personal facts, but it sometimes takes a while for the old cylinders to warm up. You may even find subtle changes in your personality." He patted his arm reassuringly. "Try not to let any obstacles upset you. But if by chance something does, feel free to call me day or night. Either way, I count on seeing you next Saturday after your physical therapy session."

"Is Kate bringing Bonny?" Jared asked, reverting to his priorities.

Glenbrook sighed in exasperation, but was secretly pleased. "I think so. But as I explained, the child won't be allowed up here."

"I know, I know." Jared swung his powerful legs over the edge of the bed. The movement hurt, but he still couldn't help but marvel at his new dense thighs and calves. He felt a little like Clark Kent transformed to

Superman. "If I hurry, I can head them off in the lobby. You ever see Bonny, doc?"

The question startled the doctor. "No."

"Well, you're missing out." Jared beamed with pride and delight. "She's smart, loving and cute. Everything a man could ever want in a daughter. If a man had the chance to be her father, I mean," he added quickly.

"Kate Reed seems like a top-notch lady, too," Glenbrook remarked, frowning as Sam took yet another peek in the mirror. It was as though he'd never seen his own face before!

"Oh, yes, she certainly is." Jared studied the play of emotion in his slanted green eyes as he thought about Kate. Because of his sad background, Sam had never allowed himself to feel anything too deeply. He should have. It gave his handsome face new mystery and appeal.

"Mrs. Reed is bound to be fragile, a new widow and all," Glenbrook cautioned with a trace of parental sternness that reminded Jared of his own late father. "She'll have her own unique set of needs, only so much strength to share."

"Yes, I'm well aware of all that," Jared replied with soft certainty. "I will be handling her with the greatest care."

The physician's brows jumped, betraying his amazement. "I'm very pleased to hear it."

Jared didn't take Dr. Glenbrook's surprise to heart. It would seem unlikely that a man like Sam would have the sense to appreciate a widowed mother who stood five foot eight in her stocking feet, with breasts and hips lush from childbearing, who spoke in complete sentences without a single giggle. She was nothing like the party girls who'd stocked this room with stuff.

All this peering at his mug wasn't going to help his credibility, either, he realized. But it was important to him to see traces of Jared Reed again in his reflection. And thankfully he did. The lines around Sam's mouth that had given his face a sardonic expression were all but erased.

Would Kate see the differences? Suspect something was up? How he longed to confide in her, comfort her, ease her suffering.

All she had to do was show up and listen. And believe.

KATE WASN'T PREPARED to find Sam ready and waiting in the hospital lobby. But there he was, seated in a wheelchair, clutching a bouquet of helium balloons. A smiling nurse's assistant stood by with a small duffel bag and a grocery sack brimming with stuffed animals.

"Kate! Bonny! Hello!"

Kate lifted a hand in tentative greeting, noting that a lock of black hair had fallen across his bruised forehead, giving him a helpless look. Odd, it wasn't like Sam to tolerate a hair out of place. Even stranger, he'd never before looked sincerely happy to see her. His usual playful smirk was replaced by a very appealing smile. Maybe Dr. Glenbrook was right. Maybe the accident had caused some personality changes. In any case, human decency demanded a curve to her lips as she guided Bonny across the floor, past the gift shop and admittance desk.

"Thanks so much for coming."

The sexy timbre to Sam's tone sent a shiver of delight down her spine. She bit her lower lip, suddenly feeling shy. "I parked the car in the lot," she blurted in a rush. "Didn't expect you to be so ready." To her surprise he laughed.

"As good as the service has been here, I feel a little like an escaped convict hoping for a quick getaway."

"Is this a jail here, Mommy?" Bonny asked, tugging on the sleeve of Kate's white blouse. The question brought a round of chuckles, even from the nurse.

Jared gazed at his girls hungrily. Now that they were within easy reach he had the overwhelming urge wrap them in bear hug. But that kind of thing was obviously premature. With a jerky motion, he held out the balloons to Bonny. The blond imp scooted forward, and curled her fingers around the strings with a squeal of delight.

"Oh, thank you, Uncle Sammy!"

"These stuffed animals are for you, too, Bon," he said, gesturing to the sack.

"They can live in my playhouse," the child rejoiced. "When we get a roof on."

Kate cleared her throat, shifting from one foot to another. "Well, shall we go?"

"It's policy that I wheel him to the door," the nurse said, gently pushing the chair forward.

Kate followed with Bonny, and Sam's bags. They all paused at the entrance, while Jared struggled to his feet. He thanked the nurse for everything and wasted no time wobbling through the automatic doors.

Kate was at his side immediately, touching his bare forearm. "Okay?"

"Better and better." The pressure of her fingers on his skin sent a delicious heat through his system, awakening his desires with a zing. He could only imagine what real sex would do to him.

Kate gestured to a seat near the curved drive. "You and Bonny can wait here while I bring the car around."

He inhaled, primed to object. "If you don't mind, I'd like to sit in the park across the street for a little while. Enjoy the sun and the company."

Kate's violet eyes widened a little and Jared winced. She had a habit of weighing people's motives too thoroughly. He couldn't handle it today of all days. Time was wasting. The first hour of the rest of his life to be exact!

Bonny intervened then, with a dose of childlike wisdom. Slipping her small hand into his large one, she said, "Uncle Sam needs some playtime, Mommy. He's been stuck in his room a long time."

"Exactly!" he said, squeezing Bonny's fingers. "Okay, Mommy?"

Kate drew a hesitant breath. "Sam, you aren't afraid to get in a car, are you?"

He was truly flabbergasted. "Of course not!"

Kate flushed over her mistake. "I only meant . . . it would be natural to be skittish. And you did turn down other ride offers."

He rolled his eyes. "It was the drivers, not the drive that I was trying to avoid."

"So Dr. Glenbrook told me. In so many words."

"Let's go over to the park and talk about it," he suggested gently. "We don't need the doctor as a go-between anymore."

The trio made their way across the busy street with the sack and tote and gaggle of balloons. Bonny lost her grip on one of the strings, sending an inflated Mickey Mouse head skyward. Jared second-guessed her impulse to dash into the traffic after it, and cupped a huge hand on her tiny shoulder. It all happened in a flash, but Kate caught the whole incident and was visibly grateful.

"Freedom. Sweet freedom!" Jared stood on the neatly clipped grass, tipping his face to the sun. Even though they were surrounded by bustling traffic and high-rises and city fumes, he'd never felt more invigorated.

Kate steered him to a slatted park bench, keeping a close eye on the dancing Bonny. "So, Sam," she began brightly, folding her hands in her lap. "You wanted to talk?"

He turned his head slowly, studying her as one would a priceless portrait full of mystery. "You cut your hair."

Kate gasped. "I what?"

He continued to appraise her, despite her fidgety discomfort. "It's about half the length, I'd say."

Kate struggled to remain collected as he tenderly brushed some wispy strands out of her eyes. Sam wasn't in the habit of touching her. "Yes, I wanted a change, something more manageable."

He nodded with a lazy appreciation. "Looks real nice."

"Thanks . . ." She trailed off, averting her gaze.

Jared felt his confidence slipping and took a shaky breath. There were so many things he wanted to say, sentiments he longed to express. The emotional impact of this reunion was almost more than he could bear, however. His throat was contracting, lodging a rush of words halfway up his throat. He wasn't sure he deserved this second chance with her after his fatal mistake in judgment, and the enormity of his good fortune threatened to swallow him up. Where to begin? he wondered. She was waiting for him to speak, take the lead.

"I can't tell you how sorry I am for everything, Kate," he ventured with awkward sincerity. "For all the grief the accident must have caused you."

Kate had steeled herself for the onslaught of alibis. This contrite approach caught her off guard, piercing her heart like a honey-coated arrow. "It has been tough." Her eyes traveled to Bonny, weaving through a scattering of bushes. "The Helsers have helped. They've been around a lot. Their fussing has been surprisingly nice. Especially for Bonny. She adores them both and doesn't mind when they baby-sit." She flexed her hands in her lap. "It's very important to me that Bonny feel secure."

"Girls of all sizes need comfort sometimes," he couldn't help but observe pointedly.

His velvet tone washed through her veins like a dose of warm brandy. But her system had been chilled too long to completely thaw. "But growing a thick shell is part of being an adult, isn't it?" she countered in a firm but pleasant tone. "Learning to manage losses. Make do."

Since when? Jared wondered, secretly appalled. They'd always been a couple of dream chasers. Her strange attitude fueled his courage. He had to get a clear fix on her new state of mind or he'd bust! "I suppose you're very busy these days," he prompted.

"Very," she confirmed, her eyes straying to Bonny, now doing a balloon dance around a group of hospital employees seated in the shade of an oak tree. "Labor Day's just around the corner, then it's back to school for both of us. My teacher's tenure is more important than ever and Bonny will be—"

"Starting full-time days in the first grade," he supplied proudly.

"Why, yes, Sam," she marveled appreciatively. "And it's very important that we establish a smooth routine."

"How has she taken the loss?"

"She refuses to accept it," Kate lamented. "Has a childlike faith that Jared's going to return."

It took all his self-control not to whoop for joy. Bonny's mind was like a little sponge, open to all sorts of signals in the air. And he'd been sending out signals like crazy from the confines of his hospital bed.

"I blame myself," Kate went on with terse practicality. "The night of the accident, when she was running a fever, she kept waking up, asking for her daddy. I kept saying he'd be home soon, over and over again, until it became almost a chant." She blinked, her black lashes dewy. "Now she cannot seem to separate yesterday's promise from the realities of today!"

"If it's any consolation, he came to understand he'd made the wrong decision about the trip."

Kate sniffed and dabbed her nose with a tissue. "Doesn't really matter much now."

"But it should!" he objected passionately. "Jared couldn't get his mind off you. And your news . . ." His eyes lowered to her belly, concealed beneath a loose-fitting blouse.

Kate smoothed her top, uncomfortable with his stare. Had she overestimated his new concerned front? Was he reverting back to visualizing her naked? No, thankfully his expression was unmistakably sweet when he captured her eyes again.

"Would you like to tell me the news?" he asked earnestly.

"Not really," she said in quick dismissal.

"Bet I can guess."

Panic flashed in her eyes. "Please don't."

He wagged a finger at her. "You're teasing me."

"No, I'm not!"

What was the matter with her? he wondered. Maybe she was afraid he wouldn't care enough, and his luke-warm response would spoil her joy. But that didn't make sense. Despite his faults, Kate knew Sam was crazy about Bonny. "Now, Kate," he said mildly, "don't you think I'd want to join in the fun?"

"Fun?" she repeated dazedly. "What are you talking about, Sam?"

"About your pregnancy, naturally!"

She reared back on the bench as though he'd slapped her. "Where did you ever get an idea like that?"

"From your husband, of course!"

She shook her head with force. "I never told Jared anything of the kind."

His jawline sagged, his heart hammered in alarm. "But he put two and two together..."

She rolled her eyes. "That's an ironic choice of words."

"Huh?"

"I mean, it takes two to make a baby," she clarified huffily. "And we didn't get together much during his final months. Understand?"

He regarded her blankly. "You mean, you're not? You're absolutely sure?"

She chuckled softly over his disappointment. "Think back. You were with him more than I was. Sadly, by the time of his death, Jared had all but lost track of what it meant to be a husband."

"Did not!" he argued hotly.

"Did so." Her soft brows furrowed in a frown. "Jared was preoccupied even when he was home."

His mouth fell in a glum line. "Sorry. He just sensed the news was something big."

"In a way it was, Sam." Her chin wobbled, but she held it high. "I intended to ask him for a divorce."

"A what!" Sam's voice was so loud that it made them both jump.

Kate looked around, embarrassed that a few heads had turned their way. "Keep it down. Please."

"He loved you so much, Kate," he said in a quieter tone. "It seems impossible that you didn't know it."

She hung her head, fumbling with her tissue. "I would've given him a chance to explain, of course. But my mind was made up."

"You can't mean it."

She sniffed with a shadow of a smile. "Oh, Sam. Uncomplicated, naive Sam."

"I am not naive!"

She regarded him with open pity. "Relationships are multilayered affairs. Trouble seeps in slowly, and with time saturates everything."

"But you were the center of his universe."

Kate shrugged. "Looking back, you must have felt you were winning the tug of war for his attention."

Sam was a pain about that sometimes, Jared inwardly conceded. But it had honestly been business that had kept him the most preoccupied: The time spent on the museum robbery, then the catch-up cases to keep their income steady. Never in his wildest nightmares had he guessed that Kate didn't understand his goals.

"Our male friendship was important," he admitted slowly, trying to be realistic, "but a far second to your marriage vows, believe me."

"I was being gradually and systematically shut out," she insisted.

"Oh, no, Jared didn't mean for anything like that to happen."

"But it happened." She reached over to pat his huge, trembling hand. "Marriage is a partnership that needs constant renewal. Without nurturing, it all crumbles away."

Jared absorbed the truth and its consequences like a painful injection of hemlock. "You were really at the end of your rope that last night, weren't you?"

"Yes," she replied haltingly. "I desperately needed Jared to tell me that I couldn't stop loving him. That it was an impossibility."

"It was a blasted impossibility!" His voice was thundering all over again, but he had no desire to control it.

She smiled wanly. "I don't know, maybe fate just took over. Maybe Jared was meant to die without ever knowing how I truly felt."

Jared desperately, fervently, wished he'd done just that.

4

"ARE YOU SURE you don't want to have dinner at our place?" Kate twirled slowly around Sam's small living room and realized he'd disappeared. "Sam?"

"He went down there with his suitcase," Bonny told her, pointing to the cramped apartment's only hallway, which led to the bedroom and bath.

Kate gave her daughter's soft curls a pat. Bonny's intermittent yawns and shuffling steps showed that she was wilting by degrees. Kate empathized. Two hours had passed since they'd picked Sam up at the hospital, and the experience had knocked the emotional wind right out of her. First he'd shocked her by being downright sweet and attentive, then he'd lapsed into a dark funk. She hadn't believed him capable of such a range of emotion.

"What's this, Mommy?" Bonny had paused by the window facing the street to look at a lava lamp filled with green liquid.

"An antique from the sixties," Kate replied absently. "Daddy and Sam were boys back then, and liked to remember those days."

"Oh," Bonny said with new understanding. "That's why I keep my furry bunny on my bed, too. To remember the good old days at nursery school, way before kindergarten." She turned at the sound of Kate's soft laughter. "That's not funny, Mommy."

"I'm amused because you're so cute."

Bonny's round face crinkled in thought. "When I was afraid to go to school, Daddy made the bunny talk about it. I sure miss Daddy. I can't wait till he comes home and calls me his Bonny bunny again," she confided, turning back to touch the lamp with inquisitive fingers.

Kate shook her head, indulging in a huge heartfelt sigh. Bonny's denial about her father's death, her childlike faith that he would return, was a powerful force to reckon with. "I've told you many times, honey, Daddy is in heaven."

Bonny' s little back stiffened. "I feel like he's really close, Mommy. Can't you tell at all?"

Kate hadn't felt even a niggle. But she hadn't made an effort, either. She was too busy with daily routine, and obsessed by night with charting their future. Feeling fidgety, she began to wander the cramped space. She ran a finger over the maple coffee table and television set, and was impressed to find them dust free. Sam's cleaning lady, Ida Turner, had called her right after the accident for guidance, and Kate had suggested she come in and spruce things up on Thursdays, as always. It had been another reminder of how alone in the world Sam was. The Reeds were the only alternate number Ida had.

Kate stared down the dim hallway again, suddenly wondering in a panic if he'd fainted or something. "Sam! You all right?"

Sam wobbled out of the bedroom, eyeing her dazedly. "Thought you'd left."

Kate's heart pinched. How could such a vital personality fall to these depths so hard and fast? He'd seemed fine in the park. Until she'd told him of the divorce. After that he crumpled like a crisp autumn leaf.

Why would Sam take it so hard?

"Food," she pressed with forced lightness. "You need a nice hot meal. It isn't too late to change your mind and come home with us."

He leaned a solid shoulder against the painted white door frame. Despite his size, he looked pathetic. "I'm not very hungry right now. And I'm too beat to go out."

"Then we'll just have to feed you here, I guess."

"No," he objected hoarsely. "You don't have—"

"You can't let your emotions sway you from good common sense."

He stared at his feet, struggling to control his volcanic fury. "I know what I need, Kate!" *I need you to tell me you love me. I need to hear you say that you didn't mean the things you said.*

"You will eventually sort things out," she went on confidently. "But you're bound to be on a roller coaster for a while. Heaven knows, I am. I have my good days and my bad ones. But I follow old habits to keep sane. And your body needs care no matter what." She brushed past him into the tiny nook of a kitchen to open the refrigerator door, and crouched to check the contents. "Looks like Ida stocked a few things—milk, cheese, salad fixings." She straightened to inspect the freezer. "Plenty of meat up here. Bread and microwave dinners, too."

He was beside her suddenly, his fingers curling around her upper arm. "Would you please go now?" he ordered roughly. "I need to be alone, to think."

She gasped, finding it difficult to breathe. He was so large and intense, making the cramped space of the kitchen impossibly tight. "It'll only take me a few minutes—"

"I can manage!"

The unexpected release of her arm sent Kate stumbling back into the counter with a thump. She straightened her spine, primed for rebuttal, when his expression stopped her cold. He was touching his mouth, as though shocked by the volume of his voice. And his eyes . . . The sea green glitter she was used to was replaced with something much darker in color and depth. As if the lights had gone out in a dense forest. Raw despair was mirrored there with the sharpest clarity imaginable. As though he'd traveled through a tunnel of fear and pain.

But hadn't he? The accident. The loss of his best friend. Those weeks in a coma. Where had he really been all that time?

There were so many things she was curious about, but this wasn't the time to probe. Whatever was troubling him was too fresh. The man she'd perceived as a pesky manipulator was suddenly volatile, and taking her more seriously than he ever had before.

Amazingly, she seemed the fuel for his fury.

"Is there anyone else I can call for you, Sam?" she asked in a nervous hush. "Anyone you'd rather—"

"There is no one else! But thanks just the same," he added, averting his gaze. She had flinched as if frightened of him! Just when he didn't think things could get any worse!

"We'll be on our way, then," she said a bit shakily. "It's getting late." Kate collected Bonny and her purse, then turned abruptly with an unguarded look of sympathy and determination. "I know you must feel your whole world is caving in around you right now. But you're tough. You'll make it. We lose, but we go on, rebuild and heal. One day at a time."

Jared stared blankly as his reason for living closed the door firmly behind her. Despite her kindness, there was a measure of distance in her tone. As though her plans for rebuilding her shattered life were in progress, going full-speed in a new direction. One day at a time, yes, but she was so many days ahead of him. If he was going to recapture what they once had, he would have to hurry. But where to begin, when he wasn't even sure why she wanted to leave him in the first place?

He'd been cautioned that the road back was bound to be rocky. But maybe it was closed completely, beyond repair.

To think he'd perceived himself the devoted husband, about to become a father again! How in heaven's name had he gotten it so wrong?

"LOOK WHAT THE JUNKYARD dog dragged in!" Eve Kemp looked up from her computer screen Monday morning as the door to Valley View Investigations swung wide open and Sam Stone's large, lean form eased through it.

"It's what the cat dragged in," Jared corrected.

"No ordinary house cat could handle a panther like you," she returned saucily, savoring the sight of her boss dressed in a pale blue cotton shirt and jeans, as well as his trademark black leather jacket and boots.

Jared relaxed a little. Finally, a friendly face who would've been happy to see Jared or Sam anytime. "Manage to keep the place afloat?" he asked.

"Ha! As if you even wondered, lover boy."

As if he had. More than one person had mistaken the skinny little mite in her twenties, with a cap of hair too red to be real for nothing more than a lightweight contender. But nothing could be further from the truth. Eve was an office organizer extraordinaire, the glue, the spunk, the constant force that kept Valley View going year after year, no matter what Jared and Sam managed to get themselves into.

Eve swiveled her chair away from her computer screen, and tracked his stiff journey to the coffee machine. She pushed up the sleeves of her coral top, and planted her freckled arms on the reception desk. "What are you doing here, anyway?"

He shrugged his broad shoulders. "It's a Monday, right? We're open for business." Nosy Eve would question his every move. And being a bohemian who thrived on mysticism, she'd probably gobble up his story as a fanciful child would a fairy tale. But he couldn't tell her the truth yet. Kate had to be the first to know. If he never had the opportunity to tell his wife, the secret might very well remain his alone forever.

Kate's motto—One Day At A Time—frequently replayed in his head. But he'd spent the weekend closeted away in Sam's cramped quarters, surviving on the food that Ida had left, and the future seemed impossibly bleak. He'd taken intermittent naps, hoping that he'd eventually wake up in his old life, anxious to tell his wife all about his crazy nightmare.

No such luck.

He was learning all too quickly how lonely a number one really was. Jared's idea of the way to start the day was a blend of happy commotion: Bonny tearing through the house with an armful of her dolls, singing along with a blaring television; Kate moving around the kitchen, clinking silverware, pouring juice and brushing up against him as he sat at the table reading the newspaper.

His only early morning distraction on the weekend had been a playback of Sam's telephone messages. He'd set the answering machine on the kitchen table beside his bowl of cornflakes and had turned up the volume, primed to catch anything that might help him in his search for the creep who'd set them up. Ida Turner, bless her efficient little soul, must have even flipped the tape at the proper time, which had given him a full sixty minutes of air time. He'd felt like an eavesdropper as a string of cooing intimate messages from Sam's ladyfriends filled the air.

Ultimately he concluded there were no leads there to cull. Except perhaps from the one voice that kept popping up with regularity, that of a Gretchen. She had assumed that he was checking his messages and offered over and over again to pick him up from the hospital. Her tone eventually got downright crisp, as though she were the injured party.

Did she have the right to be put out? Had Sam made her some promises? He'd found some lingerie and toiletry items scattered around, and a few tops hanging in the closet. Not enough stuff for a live-in, but definitely an overnight guest. A busty guest with blond hair and a preference for sweet floral cologne. He wasn't looking forward to it, but Gretchen's motives would have to be investigated.

He gazed over at Eve, in the process of saving whatever she'd written on the computer screen. He wanted to question her about a lot of things, but would have to do so subtly.

"It's hard to believe you're ready for work," Eve objected. "You were just sprung from the hospital."

"Yeah, but I've been awake for two weeks, in a grueling physical therapy program." He lifted the carafe from its hotplate, clinking it against his mug as he poured some of steamy brew. "So, Kate tell you I was being released?"

"No, Dr. Glenbrook did. A few of your, uh, ladyfriends and I got to know him during your recovery. Though things did get a little testy in the end when you finally woke up and no longer allowed visitors."

"I'm sorry, Eve, but if he let you in, he'd have had to let the cops in, too. We sort of conspired to give me the space I needed to heal."

"Oh, well, that makes me feel better. As far as Kate's concerned, I did speak to her yesterday," she said a little too sweetly. "To find out why you weren't answering your damn telephone!"

"Sorry about that." It was amazing how easily little Eve could make a man feel sheepish. "I suppose Kate painted me a monster in his den."

"Well, she did say you were out of sorts."

Jared stared at the pale green wall, struggling to keep control. "She was no better, dissatisfied with me, the business, her marriage. Never realized she took my rivalry for Jared's time so seriously."

"Truths have a way of coming out once it's too late."

"There has to be a lot more to her discontent that I don't know about. Details I don't have." He stopped and remained silent, hoping Eve would jump in.

"I'm sure there is," she agreed. "I've known she was unhappy for quite some time—"

He was horrified. "You knew and said nothing!"

"Girl talk is supposed to be kept confidential!" When his shoulders slumped, she lost her steam and sighed. "Hey, don't let her threat of separation rattle your conscience too much—"

"She said divorce!" He half turned, his profile granite. "She find another man?"

"Heck, no!" Eve hooted in disbelief. "She's way too busy. Besides, I can guarantee her complaints would've fizzled into nothing had Jared lived to hear them."

"Why, Eve? I found her very convincing."

She looked disgusted at his ignorance. "Because Jared was even more convincing. He would've knocked the wind out of her with some grand passionate play and she'd have been too weak to walk anyplace."

He turned to face her slowly, mounting hope softening his features. "You really think he had that kind of magnetism?"

"Sure," she insisted with implicit faith. "Underneath that ordinary body lived one of the most vital, exciting men I've ever known. Why, he was just the kind I'm searching for myself," she confided dreamily, eyeing the entrance. "He'll come through that door one day and I'll know him. He won't have your Jean-Claude Van Damme looks or lots of money in the bank. But it won't matter cause he'll have an attitude. That indefinable something that makes guys twice his size think twice about hassling him, makes women wonder what's ticking behind his expressive eyes."

He puffed out his chest with new confidence. He was sounding pretty good after all!

"What went wrong between the two of you on Friday?" Eve probed. "Your asking for her help seemed like such a good sign, a way of the three of us remaining friends and keeping this agency on even ground."

He waved his hand in a dismissive gesture. "I had plans, things to say. And suddenly, it was all wrong."

"Like what?"

As if he could explain! He closed his eyes in a defensive reflex, fearful that his soul was mirrored there in all its vulnerability. "If she throws in the towel, wants out of the agency, everything will crumble around us," he said, choosing a truthful yet mild angle.

Eve's chair wheels squeaked as she stood. She circled around the furniture to place her hands on his rigid back. "Not gonna happen. No matter how confused she might be right now, she's too smart to give up her interests here. She knows you can't buy her out. And any income she could skim off of Jared's interest in Valley View is bound to come in mighty handy."

So true. They'd built their life-style around their dual incomes. Her schoolteacher's paycheck alone wouldn't stretch far enough to cover their monthly expenses. The house she loved so well would be the first to go. More pain in her future. All because of him.

In one of his bleaker, middle-of-the-night moments in Sam's bed, he'd weighed the idea of moving on, selling the agency, handing the cash to Kate, leaving things be. It would be the simplest plan if he could stop loving her.

But, dammit, he couldn't stop! His feelings for her were flooding his system, mounting with ear-ringing pressure until he thought he'd explode. If he couldn't fix things, he'd surely die of internal combustion.

"You caring this way, Sam," Eve marveled close to his ear. "It's real nice."

His mouth curled cynically. "A nice surprise, you mean?"

"Not really," she objected. "Well, maybe so. But there's no need to kick yourself around this much. It's never too late to grow, to change."

Jared thought Eve might tip her head into the expanse of his back, as she sometimes did during rocky moments. Instead she gave him the Sammy treatment, a pinch on his rear end! He'd have to cure her of that. "Let's snap out of this wishy-washy business and get down to business," he suggested.

"Good for you." Eve circled him as he dropped two sugar cubes into his cup. She solicitously stirred the brew with a plastic stick, a frown creasing her forehead. "Since when do you sweeten your coffee, Sam?"

"Oh." An old habit expected only of Jared. "The, uh, doctor suggested I take in calories," he improvised slowly, cringing as she dumped in a stream of unwanted cream, Sam's old favorite. "The nurses started it, got me hooked."

"Speaking of addictions, you have some gifts from well wishers back in the office. Candy and cards mostly." She wrinkled her nose. "Some of the envelopes were dipped in perfume, I swear. Lots of it dimestore cheap."

"Guess your dimestore nose has its advantages, Eve." It felt good to smile, to tease her a little. The hospital staff had been so careful with him, as though he might shatter. He sipped his coffee, avoiding direct eye contact. "So, uh, Gretchen been pestering you?"

"A little," Eve replied crossly. "Seemed mighty put out that I didn't see her as a VIP, privy to your condition and all."

"That's how she sees herself, a VIP?"

"Yeah, acted like your one and only true love ever. Considering you'd been seeing her for only a few months, I thought that was pretty nervy."

Jared turned over the information in his mind. The fact that she'd showed up shortly before the accident, and had kept close tabs on Sam's condition, gave him real fuel for speculation. Had she set him up? If so, why? And why would she hang around now?

Maybe she'd been in on the museum robbery and had been sent to find out if Sam still had his nose in the case. Sam alone had been the one in the media spotlight in the agency's search for the missing jewels. And Sam liked to boast and would've confirmed her worst fears.

Maybe Gretchen was still around now because she believed Sam hadn't died as planned.

That, and the fact that he didn't even have a clue about what she looked like, sent a chill down Jared's spine. "So she ever confront you here at the office?" he asked as nonchalantly as he could manage.

"No, thankfully!" Eve threw her hands up in exaggerated glee.

Jared tried to mask his disappointment. "You never got a look at her then?"

"Once. At the hospital. Big boobs, fluffy blond hair, pouty Marilyn Monroe lips." She rolled her eyes. "And I've heard her squeaky little voice on the telephone more often than I'd like, thank you very much!"

Jared was relieved. At least he'd know her if she crossed his path.

Worry lines fanned her eyes. "You aren't serious about her, are you, Sam?"

"Whatever I felt is long gone."

"Good, cause I think you can do better."

He nodded solemnly. "I'll try."

Eve was right on his heels as he opened the door leading to the space he and Sam had shared. With sleepwalker numbness, he headed straight for his old desk on the left.

"Whoa, where you goin'?" Eve grasped his elbow.

"Huh?" He blinked into her steady brown gaze. Another mistake! "Thought I'd sit in Jared's place for a while." He gestured to Sam's desk, heaped with the kind of novelties he'd received in the hospital. "That clutter is a waste of time. Do me a favor and go through it all. Open up the mail, sort it for me—"

"I left it because it's personal. You always say—"

"Never mind, Eve." His baritone boomed in the small room, a reminder that he'd have to fine tune the volume of his new voice. "I've lost so much time already," he went on quietly. "It's important that I get back to work, make this a real business again."

"Yeah, right." Eve nodded her bright red head in approval. "I can groove with that."

"Put the cards in an open stack—"

"What if some have cash inside?"

"Write the amount in the card and put it in the office kitty. I figure it's pretty low."

"True. It's going to be a struggle to get back on our feet financially."

Jared sank down into his old chair, and glanced at the desk calendar, still lying open on the day of the accident. He'd jotted down "retirement party for Walter, and special time for Kate." He quickly flipped it ahead. "You're owed back wages, aren't you, Eve?"

Eve lifted her chin. "Well, yeah. But I'm sort of hoping you'll eventually take me on as your partner, so I'm willing to wait."

Jared's eyes widened. "Think you're ready for gum shoes, eh?"

She placed her small hands on the neat desktop, bringing her nose inches from his. "I'd be great. I know the streets of Denver like a cabbie, am adept at drawing out people. And there's my bubbly red-hot secret weapon, too!"

"Your killer coffee?"

"No, my Gypsy blood! It gives me razor-sharp intuition. A lot like Jared's." She snapped her fingers in his face. "When something isn't balanced, I pick up on it, just like that!"

He stroked his chiseled jaw pensively. She was a master at sizing up a situation, and a walk-in client. And he would want a partner. "It just might work out."

"Yes!" She jumped up with a whoop.

"Let's begin on a trial basis. See if we can keep this place afloat between us. Now, please," he beseeched, gesturing to the other desk, "dig into that stuff and move it on out of here!"

They worked side by side with professional diligence. Jared pored over their open case files, which consisted mostly of background checks, deadbeat parents, and some title searches. He conferred with Eve on each one, and made notations for further action. It was going to take time to get through them all. Even more time to solve them all.

Lunchtime rolled around quickly. Eve was just noting the time when the outer door opened and a familiar police officer from Denver's downtown station strode into view.

"Hey, Sam!" Dennis Edgerton moved into the inner office with his hand extended. "You're looking well enough. Considering the tumble you took."

Jared stood to greet the tall, beefy detective. He'd always liked him. He was a down-to-earth guy with brown hair and broad features, always on a new diet and dressed in a suit one size too small. "Good to see you, Dennis. Good to be here at all!"

"Yeah, you're one lucky bastard," Dennis blurted candidly. "Sorry about Jared, though," he added sincerely.

"Thanks. Losing a best friend is mighty tough." He sank back down into his seat.

Dennis turned, grabbed a chair near the wall and pulled it close to the desk, obviously set on an intimate conversation. He gave Eve, who was suddenly busy watering a potted yucca tree near the window, a side-long glance.

"I want Eve in on everything," Jared promptly told him. "Any agency concerns."

"You know I'm handling your case," Dennis began.

"No, I didn't."

"They wouldn't let me question you in the hospital."

"Dr. Glenbrook was very protective."

Dennis nodded in understanding. "And you were out like a light a lot of the time. But that didn't stop me from trying to piece it all together."

The thrill of the hunt. Jared could feel an old familiar hunger welling inside. He was hot on the trail of the biggest case of his career—his own murder. His green eyes glittered as he stared at Dennis. "Give me everything you have."

Dennis reached into his sport jacket and produced his small black notebook. "I'm supposed to ask you the questions, and write down the answers in here," he explained patronizingly.

"C'mon, man! At least make this a two-way dialogue."

Dennis shifted on the hard wooden chair, crossed his legs and flipped his notebook open on his knee. When Jared realized the detective was scanning his desk for a pen, he promptly supplied one.

"Okay. We've concluded that Jared was at the wheel. Why was that?"

"He was like a kid with that car. Loved to take it on the road. I was feeling kind of tired, so I let him."

"He could be as stubborn as a mule when he wanted his own way," Dennis added with a chuckle.

"He was the greatest partner a guy could ever have!"

Dennis waved his pen. "Simmer down. I've lost a few friends on the force over the years, and I find it easier to keep them in perspective, rather than make saints out of them."

Jared rolled his eyes. The last thing he needed right now was another list of his faults!

"Was Jared tired, too?"

"You mean, was he alert enough to handle the wheel?" Jared interpreted defensively. "Yeah, he was! Driver error didn't enter into this accident at all!"

"So the brakes suddenly gave out and Jared lost control of the car?"

"Right!"

Dennis worked his jaw, his tone reluctant when he spoke. "It was impossible to tell if the brakeline leak was caused by natural wear or a deliberate slice."

"Sa—" Jared halted. "I can tell you the Camaro was in peak condition. Nothing wrong with the brakes on the way up the mountainside."

"I understand why you wouldn't want to think that line needed replacing, Sam. But nobody would blame you—"

"I'm not dodging the truth! Someone tampered with that car. And we were forced off the road by one of those extended cabs, black or navy in color. Looked like a Ford, but it was impossible to tell."

Dennis took some hasty notes in shorthand.

"You talk to anybody at that tavern, Dennis?"

"Yeah, the owner, a guy named Wayne, heard about the accident. Came to us."

"Have a crew cut?"

"That's him."

"Did he say anything about seeing a truck like that?"

Dennis nodded, his eyes ever watchful.

"Did he see who was driving it?" Jared prodded.

"No. The driver never came inside."

Jared nodded in satisfaction.

"You know that's not enough to go on, Sam. There's hundreds of those trucks on the road."

"This one will have had some red paint scratches."

"Checked all the auto body places. We didn't catch it."

"The Camaro must have had scratches, too, though," Jared ventured. "Some truck paint."

"You guys scraped a lot of stuff. Brush, trees, rock."

"Any paint, Dennis?" he pressed with a tight smile.

"Black."

"All right then! So you know this wasn't an accident! Even if the brakeline was inconclusive."

Dennis exhaled as the private eye jerked forward over his desk. "Could it be that this truck driver was trying to slow you down, help you out?"

"No, it couldn't," Jared denied through gritted teeth. Why was Dennis being so impossible?

Dennis read his mood with ease. "You know the routine, Sam. I play devil's advocate, challenge every issue."

"And I walk straight into it swinging." He sat back with a heaving sigh, aware of Eve's feather touch on his shoulders. "I know I'm overanxious."

"Natural thing," Dennis said mildly.

"It was horrible," Jared confided as vivid images jumped to life in his mind. "The truck hovering in the background like a huge steel stalker waiting to pounce, charging in at our worst moment—forcing us over the edge, into that ravine!"

The detective's lips pursed in sympathy. "So, was, uh, Jared planning to take this trip all along?"

Jared was quick enough to see a hint of suspicion in Dennis's gray eyes. "Not at first, but he went along willingly."

"Business trip or something personal?"

"Business of course! You found the ruby ring, didn't you?"

"You say you guys had a ring?"

"With a stone the size of a cough drop. From the Carson Collection."

Eve gasped in surprise, her nails digging into his shoulders.

"We did find that." Dennis's expression remained impassive. "Where'd you get it?"

Jared related Sam's story about the mysterious phone call that had got the deal rolling, the agreed meeting spot, the ring arriving by messenger and the twenty grand they'd brought along for the payoff.

Dennis blinked, his mind working behind his bland expression. "Seems like a small settlement for that much loot."

"Could make sense, knowing how impossible it would be to fence that high-profile stuff without a source. You find my money?"

"Yeah, near the wreckage, still in the envelope. You'll get it back, along with the agency gun."

"So my story adds up."

"What you've told me does," he admitted. "So what happened inside the tavern?"

"Nobody showed up, as I'm sure you've deduced. Smells like a trap from all directions."

"But why bump you guys off at all?"

"To get us off the case for good?"

Dennis rolled his eyes. "One minute you're saying the stuff was too hot to fence and was being sold to you at bargain prices, and now you're saying the offer was too good to be true and somebody wanted to kill you."

The theories were in contradiction, but Jared couldn't help it. "I don't know where the truth begins and ends. Not yet."

Dennis sucked in a noisy breath. "Okay, okay. Let's just say the plan was to murder you. What would the thief hope to gain?"

"Peace of mind? We've been hitting this case pretty hard. Could've made somebody real nervous. What better way to trap us than to strike a deal with a missing museum piece as bait?"

"You should've called us in right off," Dennis said grimly. "The thief's up for murder, you know. Killers don't deserve deals."

"We weren't going to let him get away," Jared said defensively. "We were more than capable of making the collar."

Dennis, taking copious notes, shifted in his chair. "Have to admit you've given me some things to think about."

Sam's deep laugh filled the room. "Why, if I'd not lived to tell the tale, you might have thought I had all the jewels stashed someplace!"

Dennis chuckled along halfheartedly. "You realize you haven't even asked about your car or its contents?"

Sam would've probably asked about it first thing. "Oh. Sure. Is it salvageable?"

"Nope."

"There might have been something useful inside though," he recalled pensively.

"What?" Dennis nearly jumped out of his chair.

"Well, there was a map to the tavern. It came with the ring." He stopped abruptly as Dennis deflated before his eyes. "Don't look so disappointed. It's a big deal. It was drawn by our killer, most likely. You might be able to lift some fingerprints from it, or get a lead from the printed directions on it."

"We didn't find any map. Where was it?"

"First clipped on the driver's sunvisor, then on the passenger's. It really should've been there, Dennis."

"Nothing about this case is predictable." With that cryptic remark Dennis closed his notebook and prepared to leave. Jared stood with the detective.

"Thanks for stopping in, I think." His words were more lighthearted than he felt.

Dennis nodded. "Glad you made it, Sam. And...sorry again about Jared. Hope Kate and the girl, Bonny, will be okay."

"I intend to see to it," the private eye assured him.

Dennis beamed with approval. "Good man. Talk to you soon."

"Dennis, if you come up with anything, call, will ya?"

Dennis offered him a silent salute, offering no guarantees. Eve walked the police detective out, but returned promptly.

"What a crazy setup!" she exclaimed.

Jared stared down into his coffee and warmed his hands on the sides of the cup. Suddenly he was cold with trepidation. "Did you find Dennis a little curt?"

"Oh, I dunno. Played it all pretty close to the chest, I suppose, if that's what you mean."

Jared nodded. "It was cat and mouse all the way."

"That's procedure."

"Yeah, sure. But you know, Eve, I felt like he was leading me around on a very short leash."

Eve frowned in thought. "Like he had the answers and was testing your honesty?"

"Yes. There was a grim smugness about him. I have the feeling he believes he's close to solving this."

"Where was he leading with those car questions?"

"I have no idea. Too bad that map got away. It was a tangible lead, something to back up my version."

Her eyes squinted in determination. "We can beat him to the punch if we have to, together—as a team!"

"It will be a defensive course all the way," Jared predicted. "A race to put events in proper perspective before the police have a chance to twist them wrong. I wonder if you understand how tough the going might get."

She huffed in disgust. "I get it, Sam. We're out to save your ass!"

His mouth curved affectionately. "You know I want you along, Eve. But this particular case is so dangerously close to home, it may be the wrong one for you to cut your teeth on."

"Don't you get it? That's why I need to be in on it. Because one of our own went down." She sniffed, her eyes moist at the edges.

Jared's heart lurched. His best friend was rarely out of his thoughts. How he missed him! Of course he had the advantage of knowing that Sam had a whole new and challenging destiny to face someplace else. That made the loss a little easier to take. "Okay, Eve," he said in surrender. "You're in all the way. Hopefully, as we try to 'save my ass,' we'll recover the Carson Collection in the process. That will mean half the reward comes your way."

"Hope you'll understand, Sam, that I want to give my share to Kate, for Bonny's future."

"I do understand, kiddo. We're already thinking as one, like good partners should."

5

EVEN THROUGH the chipped windshield of Eve's old blue Mustang, his old home never looked better to Jared. It was Tuesday afternoon. He and Eve had been out on the road, following a lead on one of their open cases, when he'd offhandedly suggested they drop in on the Reeds. To his relief, Eve had agreed without her usual barrage of questions.

Jared had mustered the courage to question Kate further about her divorce plans and wanted to strike quickly before he could reconsider. He was certain he wanted to fight for his old place, but couldn't begin to battle something he didn't understand. Besides, how awful could Kate's side be? He'd been a decent husband. But it wouldn't be a picnic, either; she'd again believe she was speaking to a third party about their troubles and was bound to be blunt.

Nostalgia warmed him as he took a long look at the familiar suburban home. The housing development was located in the open, rolling land outside the city. The one-level ranch-style homes were made of timber and stone, with huge glass panes to offer glorious views of the Rocky Mountains and endless acres of tranquil farmland. It had been his heaven on earth. Hopefully a man could go home again.

Jared eased out of the passenger door, and Eve quickly joined him on the driveway, the clogs on her small feet clattering noisily.

"You seem kind of nervous, Sammy."

"Is it that obvious?"

She inspected his face up close. "If you could just stop twitching your eye, you might not look so, well, volcanic."

He muttered a string of oaths worthy of the original Sam Stone.

Eve laughed. "Look, we're all friends here. And friends forgive and forget, don't they?"

"You have a point," he murmured thoughtfully. Eve was saying more than she realized. Sam and Kate had been the best of friends for years. What could be smarter than moving in on her from that angle first? It would lessen the risk of scaring her off with his new and sudden interest.

"I'm sure you can patch things up easily, sugar buns." She reached down to pinch his butt as they walked up the two shallow steps leading to the front door. He quickly intercepted her itchy fingers. Sam had always loved to flirt with her, but Jared couldn't handle it. He still felt married and her intimate words and touch made him uncomfortable.

"If you're really interested in a partnership, Eve," he said with sudden inspiration, "you're going to have to shift into low gear. The chummy tweaks and nicknames were fine for a colorful receptionist, but associates have to appear professional."

Eve jabbed the doorbell, then tipped her freckled face to his. "Does this mean no more sex?"

Sam and Eve had gone that far! Jared swallowed and nodded.

Eve squinted. "Hmm...that time you spent in a coma must've done some crazy things to your head."

"I'll tell you all about the trip sometime."

There was no reply to their ring, but the garage door was standing open and both the van and the Lumina were there.

Everything had to be all right. Didn't it? Jared stomped back down the steps across the concrete apron and into the garage, faster than was comfortable for his achy joints. Cutting between the vehicles, he moved to the service door in back. He released a sigh of relief. He could hear feminine laughter coming from Bonny's playhouse. The project had been about halfway to completion before the accident. The bare walls needed siding and the roof was just a hollow frame. From this distance Kate's head was barely visible through the roof as she moved around inside.

"Occupy Bonny for me for a while, will you?"

"Sure." Eve ran ahead, waving her hand above her head. The small figure in a bright paisley dress, full of free-spirited bounce, could've easily been mistaken for one of the neighborhood girls. Jared took his time, sauntering through the grass, ducking under some low tree branches. To his delight he was now tall enough to easily peer at the little house's inhabitants through the framed roof. The ladies were setting up a tea party on Bonny's plastic dining table.

Bonny's blue eyes grew huge at the sight of him and she screamed in surprise. "Sorry, Uncle Sam," she peeped as his face crumpled in hurt, "but I thought you were a monster, blowing my house in."

He laughed then. "What you need is somebody to finish up this place, make it monster-proof."

Her curly head bobbed matter-of-factly. "It's my daddy's job."

Jared beamed in pleasure. He could see that the child's statement disturbed Kate by the scowl on her face as she set down her plastic teacup, but he wanted to think Bonny could sense his presence. Even if it was plain old denial, he hoped that it would make the truth easier to swallow when the time came. "So, Kate, have time for a talk?"

She looked startled. "Yes, of course." Eve, announcing that she'd take Kate's place at the tea table, pushed her out the small green front door. Kate looked disconcerted for a moment, but recovered quickly and linked her arm with Jared's. "Actually, I'm glad you stopped by. I have some things I'd like to say to you, too."

She did? Jared stared down at her with a hammering heart. Her violet eyes were shifting with uncertainty, something that had always excited him, left him guessing. As he began a deliberate stroll toward the house for some privacy, he said, "I really would like to finish that project for Bonny. If you don't mind."

"Mind?" she repeated joyfully. "I'd be thrilled! What, with autumn closing in on us and all, I intended to hire someone."

"Consider the job done. And any others that come up."

She gave his arm a small reassuring pat, filling him with warmth. "Sam, I really want to apologize for the way I acted at the hospital. I had no right to dump on you, about the—you know, the divorce."

"Oh."

"I can tell it's upset you," she said anxiously.

He sighed in affirmation, knowing it would be an impossible bluff.

"It truly touches me that you care. And I had no right insinuating you were solely to blame—" She broke off self-consciously. "This is so awkward. It's just you keep surprising me at every turn. As though you're a whole new man."

She'd find out! Jared suppressed a smile, relaxing a little.

They lapsed into a companionable silence as they moved through the glass door leading to the family room. Kate led him up a step to the kitchen on the left. The table was positioned in front of a huge window that gave them a clear view of the backyard. Jared paused to stare outside, eager to once again putter around the property, enjoy the open spaces. The carpentry project would do him more good than his medications could.

"Chicken?" Kate's voice broke into his thoughts.

"Too often," he chuckled.

"No, I mean, salad. Want some?"

"Yes!" He sat down as she set a heaping plate and a glass of milk on the table. Oh, how he missed Kate's cooking! Jared dug into the creamy noodle dish with gusto, savoring every bite with sounds of appreciation. He was so lost in his treat, he jumped when she slipped into the chair beside him. He broke into a huge grin, rested an elbow on the table and leaned close.

"Where are we, Sam?" she asked softly. "Confidants? Rivals? Strangers?"

He gripped his fork thoughtfully. "Been all of those things to each other, I guess."

She gave a small laugh. "Mostly rivals."

"Not in a cutthroat way," he objected honestly, knowing full well that Sam had cared for her in his own fashion, the best he could. "Families compete and irritate, but they forgive and stick together. You came to get me in the hospital, even if you didn't understand. And I believe you'd have reconsidered that divorce idea." He turned to look her straight in the eye. "If there's anything I can clear up, anything I can say or do to help you put your marriage back in perspective . . ."

"I'll let you know," she quietly assured him. "I'm working things through the best I can."

"What things?" he asked anxiously. "Jared didn't know you were so unhappy. He thought everything was great." The last phrase dissolved in a disheartened grumble.

She sat back in her chair, looking deflated. "It would be very difficult for a bachelor to understand."

"Give me a chance to help you!"

Kate gasped in astonishment. "How could you possibly hope to do that?"

"By being here," he said simply. "One friend to another. What do you have to lose?" He set down his fork and squeezed her wrist. Her pulse was jumping beneath his fingers. "If, after everything's said and done, you still say you and Jared were hopeless, I'll accept it."

"*You'll* accept it?"

Damn his impetuosity! "I mean, I'll accept that you're satisfied with your conclusions," he improvised. "And I won't argue Jared's point of view anymore."

She stared at him in wonder. It had to be part of Sam's grieving process, playing the stand-in husband. It was only fair to respect it, she supposed. It was likely that he was feeling mighty guilty for all the years he consumed Jared's time with exaggerated SOS calls on cases and personal crises. "Maybe we can try and work things through together."

"Yes, that's what I want. All I ask, Kate, is that you keep an open mind. You and Bonny are the only thing I have to cling to. If you'd just believe that much. Trust me until you have reason not to."

"Okay." She took a shaky breath. "To start with, I'd like you to tell me about the night of the accident without any sugar-coating," she pleaded. "The police have been kind enough, but they behave as though I'm the one holding back!"

His man-of-the-house hackles rose. "That's downright crazy."

"It sure is to me. Walter paved the way the best he could, but even he doesn't want to discuss the nitty-gritty."

"Well, he's always been overprotective where you're concerned. But damn that Dennis with all his fishing!"

She pounded the table. "I'm sick and tired of being shielded."

Jared nodded in understanding, and went on to explain the situation with care. He outlined how they were lured to the tavern with the ruby ring as bait, but skimmed over the fatal ride down. Naturally Kate already knew the details of the museum robbery and their search for the jewelry.

"Jared didn't want to take that trip, honestly," he said in closing. "But like I told you, he thought you were pregnant, and was excited about getting the reward."

"Yes, Jared made a lot of assumptions," she said with a trace of bitterness. "So many decisions were taken out of my hands. As if it wasn't worth consulting me."

"Can you fault him for wanting to be a daddy again?" he demanded bleakly.

"No, but it's a reminder of how many nights I waited up for him, only to have him collapse in bed with a groan. Try making a baby under those conditions!"

"What about the nights you trudged in late?" he countered automatically. "Off at PTA meetings or parent-teacher interviews? Or the times he came home to find a house full of teachers, drinking your better wines?"

"But I felt I had to do those things—"

"So did he at times, Kate," he insisted gently.

"If only he'd shown up at school once in a while with a sandwich or a soda or a kiss! Brought home a bunch of flowers from a sidewalk stand downtown."

"He missed many a meal himself," he countered, "stuck at the office working late. A surprise visit from you and Bonny would've meant the world."

Her delicate jawline slacked as she absorbed the impact of his message.

"Two people too wound up in their own business. Two people," he repeated significantly.

Her face hardened. "And there were so many other little things, things that kept piling up until it was one big, enormous pain. I would've liked a sportier car to complement the van, but no, we get a boxy four-door. It just showed up in the driveway one day. I wanted to see Europe last year, before another baby, but no, we had to go to Hawaii to that investigator's convention." She thrust her finger in his face. "And you had to come along, Sam Hula-Hula Stone!"

"We had a super time! The three of us. Didn't we?"

"Depends what kind of fun you want. I wanted my husband all to myself. At least part of the time." She continued before he could as much as inhale. "And about this imaginary baby. He makes the assumption that it's in the works, decides we need that money, goes off on a wild-goose chase, risks confronting a killer and ends up losing his life!"

Jared swallowed hard as tears welled in her eyes. "Okay, so he did some major sleepwalking this past year," he croaked with effort. "Most of the trouble between you was his fault. But he never had anything but the best in mind for you. And neither one of us thought we were dealing with a killer that night. Believe me."

They sat in silence for a long thoughtful moment.

"You know what, friend?" she said finally, dabbing her eyes with a napkin.

His heart stopped beating. "What?"

"All in all, I do feel a whole lot better."

Before he knew what was happening she was resting her head against his chest. He stroked her hair with a trembling palm. "Me, too."

"Oh, if only Jared and I had backtracked just a little bit. If he'd begun to view me as a friend worth confiding in again, these problems never would've escalated."

"No, I don't suppose they would have."

She raised her eyes to his, her mouth curving. "If you get anything out of this, Sam, I hope that it's the message that you need a woman of your own to share things with."

"Yeah, yeah, maybe so."

"Just don't make the same mistakes—overworking yourself, losing sight of the good stuff."

"I'll try."

"Hope I haven't been too hard to take. I'm sure wherever Jared is right now, he appreciates your drawing me out. Even though I'm still raving furious with him, at least I have his side of the story to chew on, too."

Jared forced a smile. After all this heart-wringing, tear-jerking talk, she was still furious. How long could he possibly handle hearing this kind of criticism about himself? How long could he handle being this close without intimacy? He didn't realize how tightly he was holding her until Eve and Bonny burst through the sliding-glass door in the family room.

"What's the matter, Mommy?" Bonny scurried up into the kitchen to pry them apart.

"Nothing at all," Kate assured her, kissing her daughter's soft cheek. "Sam and I were just talking some things over and got kind of sad." She rocked Bonny against her chest and gazed over her curly blond head. "You know, Sam, you might as well take the Lumina along when you leave."

His mouth thinned grumpily. "You must really hate it!"

She gurgled with laughter at his forlorn eyes. "I just got to thinking how rough it must be for you to be stuck without wheels. And it's just going to waste, sitting there in the garage."

"All right. Thanks." He watched mother and child, locked in a gentle rhythm of their own. How desperately he wanted to cradle them both, be a part of their family once again. He wasn't aware that he was clenching and unclenching his fists on the table until Eve patted his shoulder.

"You have a nice talk?" Eve asked.

"Yeah, partner, we did."

"Oh, so you did pull off your promotion!" Kate congratulated the redhead with a twinkle in her misty eyes.

"This sounds like a conspiracy!" Jared complained, trying to appear jolly, even though he was feeling hopelessly left out.

"Eve did ask me what I thought of her taking Jared's place," Kate admitted. "You have to admit she knows her stuff."

"Suppose we better get a move on," Eve suggested, giving him a gentle nudge between the shoulder blades. "I want to get back to the office, do my efficiency thing."

Jared stood up gingerly, as the hard oak seat hadn't done his bruised body any good. Kate, in the meantime, rose to retrieve the extra set of car keys she kept on a rack near the sink. She pressed them into Jared's hands.

"I'd appreciate it if you'd have a talk with Walter about the accident," she murmured. "He may know more than he's letting on."

He held her hand along with the key ring. "If I learn anything, you'll be the first to know."

"You coming back soon?" Bonny asked, her huge blue eyes round with excitement.

He crouched to kiss her forehead. "I sure am. Together we'll get that hut in shape. It's supposed to rain tomorrow, but I'll be here first thing Thursday. The supplies for the playhouse are still in the back corner of the garage, aren't they?"

Kate nodded. "Just as Jared left them."

"You still have all his tools, don't you?"

"Kept everything but his clothes." Her mouth crooked in a sad smile. "Figured there'd be things that meant something to you, mementos you'd like to hang on to."

She hadn't been angry enough to let go of him completely, Jared realized with relief. And it was nice to know his things were intact—the silver pocketwatch from his grandfather, his collection of comic books, his high school souvenirs. "Thanks for waiting for me, Kate."

Kate's knees weakened as he hovered overhead, so enticingly close. His voice enveloped her in husky velvet and his eyes washed over her like warm green seawater. Funny, she'd never before perceived Sam as a man of insight and compassion, but now he seemed to possess both of these qualities. The revelation sent a strange and wondrous tingle the length of her spine. "There'll be plenty of time to sort it all out, I suppose," she said more to herself than anyone else.

"We'll just put that all on the back burner for now, till we're ready," he crooned in agreement. *Until I can tell you the truth and claim everything that's mine.*

Jared followed Eve down the tiled hallway to the front door, trying not to look at all the framed photographs lining the walls, pictures of his happiest times. It was tough to walk out this way, on everything he knew, everything that was his. But there was no shortcut ahead. He'd be taking the long way home.

JARED WASN'T CERTAIN if Walter Helser would still frequent his favorite pool hall now that he was off the force, but he decided to gamble that he might and drop in at Shooter's the way Sam was known to do. At the very least he'd make a statement to the city's night crowd. Sam was back, in good shape and a force to reckon with. He didn't enjoy being a target on the street, but if he didn't offer himself as bait, he'd have no chance to lay a trap or two, would he?

It was close to eight o'clock when he took a hard left against traffic into the downtown joint's back lot, and was delighted to find Walter's old Buick parked at an angle near the back door.

Jared took one of the few remaining spaces and moved slowly through the lot, picking out familiar vehicles. Considering that the place was only blocks from Metro Station, it was no surprise that it had become a hangout for cops, court reporters, station house newsmen, private eyes and snitches living dangerously.

Jared walked through the steel fire door into a room nearly as dark as the inky night outside. Light flickered from the long bar on the left, the colored-glass pool lamps hanging over the three tables on the right and a huge television shelved directly above his head. The booths up front were mere shadows from where he stood.

Walter wasn't hard to find. He was standing at the bar in the fog of his own cigar smoke, tipping back a mug of beer. He'd turned as the cool night air reached him, a reflex from his days on the beat. He stared hard into the eyes he knew as Sam's, but then the old man's mouth crooked in triumph. Walter was eager to talk to him.

"Hey, buddy!" Jared sauntered up and eased onto an empty stool.

Walter shook his hand, taking care not to grip it too hard. "How ya keeping, Sam?"

"Still kickin'."

The bartender stepped up with a friendly smile. "You, uh, drinking these days, Sam? Or they got you pumped up on medication?"

"Feel like a pharmacy, Chuck," he admitted. "Definitely make it a Coke."

Chuck aimed his finger at him in pistol fashion and moved down to the soda dispenser.

Jared waved to some of the other patrons scattered around. Their faces were alight with curiosity. But it was natural, he supposed. Sam had been a regular here, had picked up a lot of tips and leads here. The accident was of a suspicious nature. And the police were keeping a lid on the Carson Collection link, as well as any other leads they had. It was all bound to seem mysterious.

Working to affect Sam's careless manner, he slouched and grinned. "So, how's retirement, Walt?"

"Boring," Walter rumbled with some humor. "Martha's got me planting bushes and roaming garage sales and packing groceries."

"You look real good."

"Well, sure. Get ten hours of sleep every night, on top of a glass of warm milk."

"Sounds like the life of a king."

"Or a baby." He rubbed the bald spot above his ring of gray of hair. "A few more months of this kind of pampering and I'll probably regress that far!"

Jared chuckled along with him. "After forty years on the force, it must be tough not to be a part of the action. To close the door on unsolved cases."

The glint in Walter's light blue eyes told Jared he'd got the message. "You can't imagine." He turned sixty degrees in a slow, loose way, checking out the nearby patrons as he stubbed out his cigar. "Let's rack 'em up for a game. Whaddaya say?"

The table nearest the front was available, so they quickly laid claim to it. Walter selected a stick and Jared lined up the balls in the plastic rack. Walter gave the cue ball a sharp tap that sent the other balls flying over the green felt surface. Jared took a stick and sized up the situation. Walter hadn't sunk a single one. The game was definitely a sham, a chance to speak without being overheard. He passed slowly behind Walter.

"Dennis Edgerton came to see me yesterday." He leaned over, braced his hand on the table's wooden edge and measured a shot with unnecessary thoroughness.

"He was acting real cagey, like he was trying to trip me up."

"Cop's job," Walter said simply.

Jared sank a solid ball in the side pocket. "But I resent the implication. I tried to be straight with him and felt like I was sinking in quicksand."

"I heard your story through the in-station grapevine," Walter reported. "Too bad you didn't manage to recover the collection, and maybe in the process solve that whole case."

"Yeah," Jared agreed ruefully. "So you've still got good sources, then?"

Walter's snorted. "Not near as good as I'd like. Unfortunately, most of my cronies are long gone, had the nerve to grow old right along with me. It would take a real insider to get the skinny on this, though," he cautioned. "Dennis is playing it very close to the vest."

"Any reason?"

"Rumor has it he's got promotion written all over him. Sergeant's slot opening up in Vice at Christmastime."

"And I'm to be his ticket?"

Walter's expression verified it. "Nabbing a killer in a high-profile case is the magic ride up the ranks, boy, and you know it." He leaned closer. "The museum guard's death of a heart attack during the heist got a lot of public attention and sympathy. If Dennis can bring that murdering thief to justice, he'll be a hero in the media."

"Surely Dennis can't suspect that I know who the thief is," Jared muttered. "That I'd shield him."

"If it's any consolation, I think Dennis would settle for the recovery of the museum pieces if he had to. Be content as the hero who recovered the state's treasures."

"I'm not about to be his human sacrifice for the sake of a promotion."

"Don't blame you, but his line of reasoning is easy enough to understand. The robbery happened in March—five months ago—and this is the first real break in the case. He's bound to be on you like a terrier on a pant leg."

"I gave him all I had."

"But was it credible? Drunken haze memories followed by a bounce to the head?"

"My story should stack up with the facts they've uncovered," Jared insisted. "Whatever they are."

Walter's mouth thinned as he studied the pattern of balls, as though anticipating his opponent's next shot. "Seems we've got a heap of nothin' between us."

"Don't underestimate your part. I now understand his bulldog attitude toward me, his fishing expedition with Kate. He's just that desperate." Jared took another shot and missed. He couldn't help it. The emotions that surfaced on Walter's face at the mention of his surrogate daughter were dark and disturbing.

"Grilling Kate stunk," Walter bit out fiercely between his crooked teeth. "She didn't know a blasted thing to pass on about Jared. He was a sterling guy. There's no way he went sour. I tried to talk sense to Edgerton about her, but he's not giving me his ear. Just keeps warning me about muddying the waters by leaping to crazy conclusions."

"You got any crazy conclusions?" Jared demanded eagerly.

Walter took careful aim and sunk a striped ball. "Nope."

"Just thought maybe if you went over that robbery file," he pressed.

Walter leaned over the rail and took careful aim, sinking two more stripes with a clatter. "Dennis has all that info under lock and key."

"But you were first on the scene at the museum. That fact alone should make you a useful source."

"Get it through your all-too-thick skull. I'm what you'd call redundant." Walter straightened, tugging at the belt buckle lodged beneath his fleshy belly. "You're really playing like crap tonight. A lot like Jared used to."

Jared grinned. "Sorry. But so are you."

Walter nodded. "Bad move, too, since guys from the station are watchin'. And the hungry media hounds. All wonderin' if this is more than an old pal reunion." With new concentration he went on to sink every last ball, one right after another, including the black eight.

"Anybody who thinks you're out of form on any level is a fool!"

"Don't take much to play the fool, Sam," Walter returned, digging into the storage box beneath the front rail of the table for the balls. "Having Kate pick you up at the hospital makes it appear that you two are still connected somehow despite Jared's death...." He shook his head. "It was a mistake that might hurt her. The cops are liable to suspect her all over again of knowing something about the collection."

"Guilt by association, you mean?"

"Exactly. You should've stayed clear of her until your own name was cleared."

"Guess I didn't stop to think what other people might think."

"You damn well should have."

"But I had no way of knowing I'd be suspected of wrongdoing," Jared objected.

"In any case, the last thing she needs is a wolf in her henhouse!" Walter sputtered, losing his cool for the first time.

Jared blurted with genuine laughter, "Simmer down and chalk your cue. I respect Kate and only want to help her."

Walter reached for a cube of blue chalk, and ground it over the tip of his stick with unnecessary force. "As angry as I am about all this," he continued on a calmer note, "I hope you'll let the police handle it, Sam. The system has its kinks, but it works most of them out."

"I do have faith in the system—"

"Then you'll listen?" he asked hopefully.

"Staying bone idle seems extreme."

Walter's bushy brows puckered over his persistence. "Try."

Jared lifted his shoulders beneath his butter-soft jacket, schooling a mask of calm over his chiseled features. "Sure, Walt, sure," he lied. He didn't want to feel even partly responsible for another man's demise. Walter looked on verge of a heart attack himself.

Jared played Walter again and a couple of other guys that Sam was particularly friendly with. There were a few females watching Sam Stone in motion tonight. Jared recognized some of them as Sam's former dates.

What would they expect of him? Jared could feel panic climbing his throat. Some probably knew his body better than he did!

He played on, avoiding eye contact, and eventually they all drifted away.

Except for one woman. A blonde in a tight, shimmery top, seated at the far end of the bar who'd been sipping tall drinks full of maraschino cherries. As the room began to thin out near closing, she made her move, slipping off her stool like a gold Slinky toy. With all her jewelry clinking, she sort of sounded like one, too.

Jared was returning his stick to the wall rack when she oozed up beside him. His jaw sagged as she reached up and clamped his face in her palms.

"You've been very naughty, Sam," she purred.

Jared didn't doubt it of Sam for a minute. But how to answer without really answering? "All different kinds of naughty," he finally joked.

She shook her head with a click of her tongue. "Not the fun kind. There I was, waiting by the telephone with my engine running."

He froze. What the hell was she leading up to?

She made a groaning sound then that held a familiar pitch. This was Gretchen from the answering machine! The one who'd wanted to pick him up from the hospital. "I've been meaning to call," he felt compelled to claim.

"When, Sam? The last time I saw you, baby, you were out cold. And here you are, in good enough shape to bend and shoot, and . . ." She trailed off, running her fingers over the expanse of his chest.

"I'm not in that kind of shape yet," he muttered.

"Well, why couldn't I drive you home!" she demanded shrilly.

Jared exhaled, capturing her hands as they rode the ridge of his jeans. "I feel a responsibility for Jared's wife, that's why," he explained quietly, aware of Walter's interest. This bedtime scene had to beat Martha's warm milk deliveries. "Getting a ride from her seemed like a good way to check on her, okay?"

"Oh." Her mouth puckered in a garish red rosebud. "I suppose that was pretty dang nice. Gretchy just might be ready to forgive you, steel tushie."

Steel tushie? Jared gulped as Gretchen's hands escaped his grasp and slid up his shoulders, forcing a crushing intimacy. Sam had so enjoyed these clingy, overendowed baby-doll types. Jared couldn't relate, but he understood. Sam was constantly searching for affection and gratification.

She began to kiss him then. Her glossed fleshy lips and cloud of tinsel hair nearly suffocating him.

"You aren't getting away from me again, Sam Stone," she said against his mouth, turning up the volume for all to hear.

As she pressed her pouty lips against his, Jared thought about the fact that someone wanted him dead. He couldn't decide whether he preferred to tangle with a plan of seduction or destruction!

6

"KATE! WHAT A nice surprise!"

"Hi, Eve." Kate eased through the frosted glass door of Valley View Investigations late the following morning with a cheery smile, dressed in a scarlet all-weather coat moist with rain.

"What brings you downtown on such a crummy day?"

"Shopping," Kate answered brightly. *Among other things*. Her gaze strayed to the door leading to the inner office.

"He's not here," Eve told her airily. "Had some business at the courthouse and the bank."

"I know," Kate said with a laugh. "He called to check on the nail supply for the playhouse. It's you I came to see. Hoped you could play hooky for an hour or two, help me round off my classroom wardrobe." In truth, Kate couldn't imagine taking the younger woman's avant-garde fashion advice, but Eve did have a knack for understanding men; especially the pair of detectives they both knew so well. Who was better equipped to discuss the new and improved Sam?

If Eve suspected ulterior motives, she didn't let on. "I suppose the teacher would have that fashion problem to tackle, too, along with the kids," Eve quipped. "Naturally, I always looked at it from the student's point of view. Wondered how much I could buy within my mother's budget."

"So, any chance of your coming along?"

"Every chance!" Eve reached into a bottom desk drawer for her purse.

The rain was little more than a drizzle as they climbed into Kate's van parked at the curb and drove the short distance to the 16th Street Mall. They dashed into Tabor Center and rode the galleria's glass elevator up to the second floor, giggling like schoolgirls over the way Eve's tomato-colored hairdo expanded with the raindrops.

The trip went as Kate expected. They floated from store to store, Eve choosing a series of outfits inappropriate for the classroom, Kate gently rejecting each and every one. It was in a changing room at Brooks, standing in her slip, that Kate finally broached the subject of Sam. Eve, holding up two of the dullest gray suits she'd ever laid eyes on, welcomed the diversion with a gush of honesty.

"Of course I don't feel awkward discussing him behind his back! For Pete's sake, Kate, didn't we discuss you and Jared? The juicy details of your discontent?"

Kate smiled wryly. "Yeah, but he died and can't complain." She inspected the two suits as though they were entirely different. She ultimately favored the pinstriped one in Eve's left hand, and eased the pleated jacket off the hanger and over her shoulders.

"Look, our arisen Sam is a fascinating topic for a rainy day story," Eve assured her with dancing brown eyes.

Kate beamed in gratitude. "He's really changed, hasn't he?"

"Amazing what a knock on the head will do to a perfectly normal hot-blooded American hound!"

"It's all so strange, Eve. The way he asked for me right away. And his displeasure over the news of my intentions to separate from Jared." She paused, studying her ivory-tinted fingernails. "I, uh, never felt that Sam especially liked me."

"I think he's always liked you, Kate. He was just an insecure baby about Jared."

Kate stepped into the pinstripe skirt, and zipped it along her slender hipbone. "Okay, let's accept that that's the old Sam. Sort of liked me, but desperately needed Jared."

Eve nodded once. "Gotcha."

"So he wakes up, determined to make contact with me," Kate went on carefully, turning to catch her reflection at different angles. "We spend some time together, and he offers to help with household chores, man-of-the-house things."

"Like finishing Bonny's playhouse."

"Right. Could it be a simple transference of those buddy feelings? Am I to be a substitute for the best pal he lost in the crash?"

Eve's turned-up nose wrinkled. "The chemistry between you isn't even close to brotherly love, is it? I mean, yesterday at your place, the two of you were burning and quaking when Bonny and I walked in on you. It's either a dose of radiation you two caught at the hospital, or something sexual." Eve cringed, caught off guard by her own candor. "Jeez, I have a nerve!"

"I'm just relieved that you felt it, too," Kate blurted in relief. "Thank heavens. I'm not losing my marbles after all!" She ran a shaky hand through her glossy black hair. "I've been racking my brain, trying to figure it all out. I mean, why do we both feel something all of a sudden? I don't think I've really changed, do you?"

"No. It's Sammy all the way." Eve drew a hesitant breath. "In so many little ways, he's behaving like Jared."

Stirring her desires as only Jared could do, Kate silently confirmed. How amazing that Eve had led her to that plain and simple truth with so little effort. Not that it made a damn bit of sense. "But I thought I was getting over Jared," she confided in lament.

"Did you really?" Eve questioned guilelessly.

"If I was, why would I be attracted to a man behaving like him?"

"Danged if I know."

"Danged if you don't!" Kate scoffed. "You don't think I was even close to dumping my husband do you?"

Eve shook her frizzy head. "Nope. Jared would've snapped out of the rut he was in the minute he got your message, and turned you into a giddy, dopey, lovesick—"

"Okay! I got it!" Kate closed her eyes and pressed her thighs together underneath the layers of nylon and wool, as her lower body burned for carnal release. She and Jared hadn't had sex often during their final months together, but when they had ... Well, it was always good. She busily adjusted the jacket's shoulder pads.

"I hope this isn't some kind of pretense on Sam's part, just to soothe my wounds while I grieve."

"He knows you're way too smart for that," Eve said confidently.

"So let's say it's all happening. I just don't know what to do. Let it evolve or shut him out before it really begins to spin . . . out of control!"

"Please don't shut him out, Kate. At least not yet, until you have more to go on. No matter where his head is at right now, he desperately wants to help you, needs to help you."

"But it's so uncomfortable. And scary."

Eve's brown eyes danced. "That's all part of the fun."

"You know I like for things to make sense," Kate said helplessly.

"Picking at something too much can damage something magical," Eve ventured, appearing, for the first time, to be a little uncomfortable voicing her opinion.

Kate understood immediately. "Are you inferring that this is a fault in me? Being too analytical?"

"I don't really know, Kate," Eve faltered. "Jared was a detail hound in business, but in his personal affairs, he seemed to take on a broader, looser outlook than you do."

Kate thought back to the things Sam had said during their heart-to-heart chat when he'd attempted to piece together her husband's viewpoint. "Are you saying that maybe Jared wouldn't have asked why, if I had, for instance, dropped into the office unexpectedly once in a while?"

"Yeah!" Eve brightened with her insight.

"And I would've grilled him pretty good if he'd popped in at the grade school to see me?" she further speculated.

Eve snapped her fingers. "Exactly! You know how you can be."

Kate's mouth drooped poutily. "Well, let's not analyze this into the ground, okay?"

"No, let's not." Eve compressed her lips thoughtfully, then said, "If you want my opinion on what to do next—"

"Do I have a choice?" Kate gibed with a crooked grin.

"In your place, I would just relax and let him lead the way."

"Just let the magic weave without too much scrutiny?"

"Yup." Eve held the other gray suit up to her elfin figure and poked out her tongue at the drab result. "My very reliable Gypsy feelers tell me that there's plenty going on around us, things that may defy space and time."

"Oh." Kate suddenly recalled the title of the book lying on the corner of Eve's desk today: *Exploring Past Life Regression.* "You haven't by any chance expanded your meditative techniques to pick up on former lives?"

Eve sighed. "You saw my manual by Professor Arthur Pendike, didn't you?"

"Yes, I did. And I don't see why your talent for tapping into the present and future isn't satisfying enough. Do you really feel it's necessary to branch out into reincarnation?"

"You've never complained about my psychic quests before," Eve sassed. "Not when I traced Bonny's stuffed bunny to a neighbor's house, or pressed a hand to your forehead and sent you to the doctor for antibiotics, or told you weeks in advance which weekend would be the best for your hot air balloon ride."

Kate raised a hand. "Okay, you've made your point. It's just . . . well, I'm not sure I buy the past lives theory. It rattles me."

"I can't say I'm solid on it, either," Eve admitted. "But I had the irresistible urge to explore the idea and now instinctively feel content with the choice. I'm inclined to believe it has validity. And personal meaning," she added significantly.

Kate gasped in dismay as the implications sank in. "You don't seriously think that Sam and I were together in another life, that he awoke from the coma determined to fulfill some kind of destiny?"

"Well, not exactly."

"Oh, you and your open mind!"

Eve gasped. "You make that sound almost like an insult!"

Kate could feel her blood pressure rising. "I'm telling you now, Eve Kemp, I don't want you flipping through the channels of the universe to discover that Sam and I once floated down the Nile with Cleo, or helped Shakespeare with rewrites."

Eve rolled her eyes. "I won't. You're going way overboard." *And way, way too far back in time.*

IT WAS STILL drizzling when Jared entered the lobby of Sam's apartment building after ten o'clock that night. He stopped in front of the bank of mailboxes and dug into the pocket of his mist-covered leather jacket for

Sam's key chain. The chain, with a pair of fluorescent-green dice, was a bit garish for his taste. If this charade went on much longer, he decided that he'd have to replace it with a simple ring. He unlocked the box marked Stone and collected the envelopes stuffed inside. He thumbed through them and found the lot similar to yesterday's, a couple of bills, a few ad circulars and a couple more greeting cards. As long as he lived, he hoped he never saw another lavender envelope. Especially a perfumed lavender envelope. Yuck.

He trudged up the stairs to the second floor. He'd deliberately run himself ragged so he could dive into bed without dwelling on the red and black decor, the emptiness. He'd gone through the motions today, but it was just a diversion all leading up to tomorrow. Tomorrow, when he could go spend some time at the place he really called home, with the most loving pair of females a man could ever wish for.

Not that today hadn't had its interesting moments. The trip to Sam's bank had been a challenge. He'd attempted to transfer some of his late friend's dwindling savings to his checking account, only to run into trouble over his signature. Jared had done his best to imitate Sam's tall, looped scrawl, but the Stone accounts were flagged, presumably by the nosy Detective Edgerton, and the young teller, nervous over the variation in penmanship, had called over a supervisor.

Jared had soon found himself corraled into a bank officer's cubicle, with a couple of harried employees who weren't sure what to do. In a burst of inspiration, he'd suggested the supervisor call Dr. Glenbrook. After all, the doc had cautioned him to expect some changes in mood, speech patterns, things like that. It stood to reason that a thing like this could happen. Science is full of wonders.

The kindly old physician had come to the rescue. He'd explained to the supervisor that though rare, a variation in handwriting sometimes occurred in re-awakened comatose patients. That had settled the matter to everyone's satisfaction. The bank had given him a calendar, a gesture intended to placate him. Jared had thrown it in a trash bin outside. He needed no reminder of the date, the time he'd lost and the time he was wasting right now pretending to be somebody else.

Sam's front door was secured, just as Jared had left it that morning, but even as he slid the key into the lock, he could sense a presence. Ever so slowly he turned the knob and slipped inside. The place was pitch black. But it didn't take a seasoned detective to recognize that there was water running someplace. The bathroom.

Jared moved silently through the living room, dropping the mail, peeling off his coat for more flexibility.

When he reached the bathroom door, he opted for a surprise attack, and burst over the threshold. There was no one in sight, but the black flocked shower curtain was closed. He tore it aside with a rustle and a clatter that shook the rod holding up the works.

"Oh!" a feminine voice cried in feigned surprise.

"Gretchen." Jared uttered her name like an oath, and stared at her nude shape, laid out provocatively in a bed of sudsy water, her gold hair piled high atop her head.

"Rub-a-dub-dub, darling," she crooned. She lifted a leg in the air and stroked her inside thigh with a bar of soap.

"Don't you believe in knocking?" he asked, struggling to control his anger.

She giggled. "Don't you?"

He bit back a sharp reply. This very well could be a game she and Sam had played. Or it could be a ruse to cover up her real reason for being here.

"'Bout time you got home," she complained in a babyish whine. "A girl could drown in here waiting."

His eyes rested on the breasts rising out of the bubbles like fleshy mountains. Drown? With those knockers, he doubted it. He also suspected she'd jumped in the water only moments ago. Crouching at tub level, he tested the water's temperature. It was fairly warm, but her skin, though slick, didn't look like it had been immersed in hot soapy water for long. She'd run this water a while back, but she sure hadn't been soaking in it. So what had she been doing?

The wanton gleam in her eye was a clear sign that she mistook his behavior for a come-on. She grabbed his hand and ran it over her belly, deftly sliding it down to the juncture between her thighs. "Oooo, how I've missed your hands. Your long wonderful fingers."

Jared gritted his teeth as she ground his hand lower and deeper beyond her nest of springy curls. Feeling violated, he pulled his hand back to his side with a swift jerk. Sam was dead and gone, and still getting him into tight spots.

"Hey, you're not very nice anymore," Gretchen complained.

"I'm not in the mood for this tonight. Sorry."

She affected what was probably supposed to be a sultry pout. Instead her pursed lips reminded him of a squashed tomato. "How do you know till you try?"

"Give me a break, Gretchen." Bracing his palm on the edge of the tub, he slowly rose to his feet.

Indignation flamed her heavily made-up face. "Well, this is a fine howdy-do! I throw my charms at you, and you say no. Weeks without sex and I thought you'd flop right in here with me."

She was beginning to make smelly lavender envelopes seem subtle. "I'd like to be the one to tell you when I'm ready, okay?" His tone was sharp, but forcing him to touch her had been too much. Luckily her clothes were heaped atop his laundry hamper. "Get dressed, will you?"

Jared took his time leaving, and closed the door after him slowly. But once in the hallway he broke into a run, anxious for a peek inside Lady Godiva's purse.

He found the bag lying on the kitchen counter—a roomier tote than she'd had at Shooter's last night. Standing near the window for light from the street, he rifled through her belongings. He took a look at her key chain, careful not to make it jangle. He studied each key, and found one to Sam's apartment. No wonder she had gotten in so easily! In all fairness, Sam had handed out his share of keys and had most likely given it to her.

He rummaged some more, and came up with a cassette. He held it up to the window and discovered it was out of Sam's answering machine! What the hell did she want with that? He squeezed the small plastic box in his hand, possibilities tumbling through his brain. Jealous lover checking out the competition? Anxious crook involved in the museum robbery, afraid that some message could tie her to the setup in the mountains? He dropped it back into the purse, certain there was nothing useful on it. He stared down at the windowsill, and realized that yesterday's mail had ended up there, beside the lava lamp. He'd left it on the television, he was sure. Apparently she'd used the window for light, too. It was all so convenient. From this angle he could clearly see the Lumina parked at the front curb. Most likely she'd stood at this very spot, snooping while on the lookout for him. She was sharper than he realized. Smart enough to check out his new wheels last night as he left the pool hall.

He returned her tote to the counter just as the bathroom door creaked open. With stealthy movements, he eased into a living room chair, far from the telltale window spot.

"Guess I'll be going," she announced with a sniff.

Best news he'd had all day! Even though he didn't want to arouse her sexually, he couldn't afford to arouse her suspicions, either, not until he knew where she stood. "Sorry, uh, babe." Sam had called them all babe. He'd said it helped when he couldn't remember a name.

She rounded the kitchen doorway with her tote, looking gooey-eyed and appreciative. "Really, Sam?"

"Really." He almost stood up, but figured it would mean another one of those mushy kisses of hers. So he stayed seated, patting her wrist as she stroked his face.

"I'd almost think you're mental, honey, not wanting sex!" she exclaimed in one last affronted rush.

Jared dropped his eyes so she wouldn't see the laughter in them. "The doctor said I'd need time, to get all my old desires back."

Finally convinced that her charms weren't in question, she perked right up and blew him a kiss. "Guess I should be goin'. You take care now."

She closed the door firmly upon her exit, and Jared wasted no time jumping up to lock it, security chain and all. He'd replace that lock immediately. One surprise like this was enough for a lifetime—two lifetimes!

7

KATE WOKE UP Thursday morning to the sound of a whirring lawnmower. She recognized it as hers, too. Each mower in the neighborhood had its own unique sound. The Reeds was discerned by its sticky choke. She quickly turned back the covers and scrambled out of bed, tugging her cotton nightie down over her hips.

Tracking the source of the noise, Kate made a bee-line for the family room, opened the blinds, then the sliding-glass door. Exactly as she'd thought, there was Sam, plowing determinedly through the overgrown grass.

She padded out onto the large redwood deck, and waved as he steered the mower back in her direction. Cupping her hands, she shouted, "You shouldn't be doing that!"

Just as she shouldn't be standing in the early morning sunshine in a gauzy pink nightie, Jared thought with a possessive jolt. Why, the rays burned right through the sheer cotton fabric, silhouetting her form provocatively. Dammit! Jared had bought her that for his own enjoyment—behind closed doors! Didn't she have any idea how it looked from this view? He couldn't help thinking how it made Gretchen's naked exhibition as cheap as a carnival peep show. Sam was such a chump not to have seen the difference.

She had to be stopped! Not caring who she thought he was, he came to an abrupt halt in the yard and ran his hand along the side of his brawny form in an hourglass motion.

Kate stared blankly, then got the message. With a squeak of dismay she pressed the front of the nightie closer to her body to erase the shadowbox effect and tore back inside.

Her heart was pounding as she chastized herself. What had she been thinking of? She pressed a hand to her chest, realizing that the breeze had instantly hardened her nipples to peaks.

Or had Sam done it? With that strange reaction to her exhibition. He'd been scandalized. Interested, with a very hungry masculine stare, but eager to stop the show! There was no doubt about it, wind or no wind, Sam was whetting her sexual appetites with the slightest effort. He kept touching her with his eyes and she kept responding.

"Whatcha doing, Mommy?"

Bonny had shuffled up beside her, obviously fresh out of bed with her crushed curls, pillow-creased face and wrinkled pajamas.

She took a deep breath to slow her racing pulse. "Watching Sam cut the grass is all."

"Is he really going to finish my playhouse, like he said?"

Kate captured the child's soft chin in her hand. "He's going to try. I'm not sure he's as talented as Daddy, and he's bound to be sore, from his injuries . . ." She trailed off, concern in her tone. Sam seemed in such a hurry to prove himself. What was the rush?

Bonny pursed her lips pensively. "I better get dressed. He's gonna need help." She darted off toward her bedroom.

"Sweatshirt and jeans, Bon," she called after the girl. "You can always peel off layers as it heats up." A few minutes later she heard Bonny slide open the door to greet Sam.

The telephone rang just as Kate was tugging a roomy green sweater over her head. She hiked up the zipper on her jeans and tracked down the cordless phone to the kitchen table.

It was the principal of her school, Martin Flanders. Kate listened to his monotone overtures while rummaging through her wooden breadbox for a box of sugar doughnuts. She placed the glazed pastries on a plate, as she thanked him for his concern over her state of mind, and assured him that she had every intention of attending the annual teacher's roundup scheduled for that very afternoon.

Did she have orange juice? She listened absently to his plans to organize the lunchroom as she rummaged through the fridge. "Only pineapple juice." She chuckled merrily when she realized she'd said it out loud. "No, not for the lunch program. Sorry."

He remarked that she certainly did sound a lot more like her cheerful old self, and it was true. She was actually laughing again. At the small things in life, the way most people do. All because of this new Sam it seemed. Not that she was any closer to making sense of it. His presence was so subtle, like a silken parachute breaking her fall. He'd eased into the picture with a quiet strength, and made her feel attractive and vital again.

After she'd hung up the telephone, Kate lingered at the window over the sink to watch a touching sight. Sam was dragging a long plank of pine siding across the yard, one of Jared's cotton tool aprons tied to his lean hips. Bonny, an identical apron cinched to her waist, was bringing up the rear with the plank balanced above her head, chirping happily about something. This was so good for her, Kate realized. To see the completion of this unfinished project. To spend time with a strong male figure so close to her own father.

Images of Jared, working on that hut, suddenly leapt into her head. The way he aligned wood on his saw-horses, the way he dusted off his hands as he surveyed his next move. Sam, though a different physical type, almost seemed to be imitating him. He even took the tape measure from Bonny's apron pocket and the pencil tucked behind her ear. Bonny must have told him of those rituals because she missed her daddy so much. Lord help her, how Kate missed him, too!

Kate sank her teeth into her lush lower lip, fighting the stinging heat behind her lids. She'd put any reflection about Jared and their life together behind her. Or so she thought. Was it possible that she still had loved her husband, even at the end when she was about to leave him? Never in her plans for freedom had she imagined how lonely she'd be without him at her side.

She couldn't get over the fact that Jared had believed her pregnant when he died. A dreamer from start to finish. A softy who couldn't bear to let down any of his people.

The kind who'd be there in a pinch, even if it was simply in spirit.

Where did that thought come from? Kate had to admit that, like Bonny, she was beginning to again feel a sense of Jared. As though he was watching over them like always. She decided she wouldn't shut him out anymore. Like Eve had said, he would never have let her get away. And perhaps all she'd ever wanted was for him to stop her, hold her fast and refuse to let go.

If he hadn't chosen to go with Sam on that fateful night, it probably would've happened just that way, too. Damn that Jared! She whirled around and pounded the countertop. Even if he were to appear right before her, she didn't know whether she'd kiss him hard on the mouth or deliver a good sock to that familiar old kisser!

FINALLY, she was joining them! Jared looked up from the sawhorses as Kate glided over the lawn with a tray laden with doughnuts, a pitcher of juice and three plastic glasses. As sexy as she'd been in her nightie, she was still impossibly desirable in her green top and jeans. The idea that someone might come along and steal his widow away was like a steel band around his rib cage, tightening with every passing day. Time was at such a premium. He had to win her back before she drifted too far afield from their decade-old foundation.

"How did you know exactly what I needed this morning?" he greeted cheerily, nodding as he transferred a plank from the sawhorse to the stack beneath the maple tree.

Kate's eyes scrunched in suspicion, wondering if he was referring to the breakfast or the unintentional peek-a-boo show.

He turned back to her, and his tanned, chiseled face split into a huge grin as he easily read her thoughts. He was making progress. She recognized his hunger and would be forced to face her own. If she hadn't already. Surely she must be wondering why Sam was suddenly appealing to her, mustn't she?

"You really didn't have to cut the grass," she said pleasantly.

So the coward hoped to play it safe with evasive tactics. He helped himself to a doughnut off the tray between them. "I know. But you didn't answer my knock, and I didn't want to start building until Bonny was here to help."

"That's right!" Bonny chirped, patting her apron.

Kate couldn't resist gazing deeply into his eyes today, to see if perhaps she'd only imagined the new qualities mirrored there. But the truth sparkled back at her like twin emerald points of light, small reassuring twinkles of sincerity and integrity. This man's spirit was an incredible force to reckon with. An irresistible force.

Her knees trembling beneath her denims, Kate ducked inside the playhouse, and bent to set the tray on Bonny's plastic table. "How nice it will be for Bonny to have this place sealed up tight before winter," she said in loud voice. She straightened and whirled around only to run smack into Sam's muscular body. "I guess I didn't have to yell, did I?" she said in a small breathless voice.

He raised a finger to her temple to brush the fine wispy strays at her hairline. He let his finger slide down the bridge of her nose. She moaned softly and shivered a little. Embarrassed, she tried to chuckle. "Guess it's still a little cool in here."

"It's smart to bundle up a little outside. You wouldn't want to catch a chill. Or unwanted attention." There was no mistaking the significance in his tone, or the warning lift to his brow. Her accidental peek-a-boo show was weighing heavy on his mind.

"I know what you mean," she agreed, a self-conscious blush flaming her cheeks. "I was just so anxious to see you—I mean, to talk to you—" She stumbled over her words, fluttering her fingers like tiny bird's wings. She gazed out into the yard where Bonny sat astride one of the sawhorses, playing rodeo queen.

"Look, Sam," she whispered. "I'm sorry. I'm acting silly. It's just, well, you've somehow forced me to confront my loneliness. I'd convinced myself that I was meant to be on my own at this point in my life, that Jared didn't give a toss anymore. And then you woke up!" She gave him a shaky poke to the chest. "You've put a whole new spin on things—mixed me up!"

Jared could barely swallow around the large lump in his throat. This was real progress. Kate was responding to him. How badly he wanted to tell her the truth! But he was afraid it might be too soon. One thing he'd learned from this marital crisis was to pay close attention to all the emotional signposts, take nothing for granted. He wanted her completely hooked, grounded in their relationship, before he laid it all out. And that meant courting her, he realized, like he had the first time. He shifted in the tight quarters to peer out the doorway. "Bon, will you see if you can find me a bigger hammer on the workbench?"

With an excited squeal, the child bounded in the direction of the garage.

Kate mentally surveyed Jared's tool collection. "Not sure we have a bigger hammer."

"Really?" He smiled knowingly.

As her mouth sagged in surprise, he skimmed his thumb over her soft lower lip with a massaging motion. Their friendship was ready for a dash of romance.

Small electrical charges quickened her pulse as the roughened pad of his thumb grazed her lips. He was taking his time, with the sexiest, laziest smile imaginable. It seemed like a lifetime before his hand moved to rest on her collarbone. It was only then that she dared to breathe. "What are you doing, Sam?"

"Nothing," he claimed evasively with an adolescent smile. And that was how he felt, too, like a reckless teenager, high on wondrous new feelings of lust. It was easy to understand why. Kate was far more open and eager than she'd been in a good long while. Looking back, he could see how and why the tension had mounted between them. It all was so simple. It all narrowed down to dealing with the basics between a man and a woman. Maintaining a sexual awareness. Acting on impulse was bound to help. And there was one thing he'd always wanted to do, in all the years he'd known her, that his old, smaller frame had made impossible.

Kate was searching his face now with anticipation. "Tell me what you're thinking."

NO RISK, NO OBLIGATION TO BUY...NOW OR EVER!

CASINO JUBILEE

"Scratch'n Match" Game
Here's how to play:

1. Peel off label from front cover. Place it in the space provided opposite. With a coin carefully scratch away the silver box. This makes you eligible to receive three or more free books, and possibly another gift, depending upon what is revealed beneath the scratch-off area.

2. Send back this card and you'll receive specially selected Mills & Boon Temptation® novels. These books are yours to keep absolutely free.

3. There's no catch. You're under no obligation to buy anything. We charge nothing for your first shipment. And you don't have to make any minimum number of purchases – not even one!

4. The fact is thousands of readers enjoy receiving books by mail from the Reader Service™, at least a month before they're available in the shops. They like the convenience of home delivery, and there is no extra charge for postage and packing.

5. We hope that after receiving your free books you'll want to remain a subscriber. But the choice is yours – to continue or cancel, anytime at all! So why not take up our invitation, with no risk of any kind. You'll be glad you did!

You'll look like a million dollars when you wear this lovely necklace! Its cobra link chain is a generous 18" long and the exquisite "puffed" heart pendant completes this attractive gift.

YOURS FREE!

(Pictured larger to show detail)

CASINO JUBILEE
"Scratch'n Match" Game

SCRATCH HERE ?

CHECK CLAIM CHART BELOW
FOR YOUR FREE GIFTS!

T7GI

YES! I have placed my label from the front cover in the space provided above and scratched away the silver box. Please send me all the gifts for which I qualify. I understand that I am under no obligation to purchase any books, as explained on the back and on the opposite page. I am over 18 years of age.

BLOCK CAPITALS PLEASE

MS/MRS/MISS/MR _____

ADDRESS _____

_____ POSTCODE _____

CASINO JUBILEE CLAIM CHART			
🍒	🍒	🍒	WORTH 4 FREE BOOKS AND A FREE NECKLACE
🔔	🔔	🍒	WORTH 4 FREE BOOKS
🔔	🔔	🍒	WORTH 3 FREE BOOKS CLAIM N° 1528

◆ DETACH AND POST CARD TODAY! ◆

The Reader Service™

FREEPOST

Croydon

Surrey

CR9 3WZ

If offer card is missing, write to: The Reader Service, P.O. Box 236, Croydon, Surrey CR9 3RU.

NO
STAMP
NEEDED

His raven brows rose and fell, making him look incredibly roguish. "Really want to know?"

"Yes!"

"I'm wondering how it would feel to lift you up like a newborn babe."

She gasped. "You weren't!"

"I was."

"You wouldn't!"

He moved his brows again.

"You shouldn't," she persisted. "Still on the mend—" Her voice became a cry as he tucked his arm under her knees and scooped her up to his chest. Turning sideways, he dipped out of the low doorway.

As they swept back into the sunny backyard, Kate didn't know whether to hold on or try to bail out. "You'll collapse," she predicted. "The cops will say I killed you!"

He bounced her in his arms a little, tipping back a bit so her weight fell on his chest. "What a way to go!"

"I mean it, Sam!"

His mouth pressed against her downy ear. "Nobody is going to accuse you of anything. I won't let anyone harm you."

Surrendering, she put her arms around his neck, just as he began to twirl them around in a circle. Kate leaned her head against his collarbone, giddy, dizzy, aroused. It was like a merry-go-round ride, with a very sexy spin.

They moved around the yard, laughing and turning. Bonny, in the meantime, was stomping across the yard with a huge rubber claw hammer in her hand.

"Hey, Uncle Sam!" she hollered. "You're supposed to be workin' for me!"

He finally ran out of steam, and gently set his soft sexy bundle back on the lawn. Every muscle in his body ached, and with a telltale groan he tumbled down to the bed of grass, and lay out flat on his back. Kate fell alongside him. So did Bonny, like a frisky little puppy.

"You wear him out, Mommy?" she asked, pressing her small fingers into his wrist. "Better not. I had him first."

"I'm fine," Jared assured her, cracking one eye open. And he meant it. Lifting his wife so effortlessly was a fantasy fulfilled. He sat up, leaned back on his elbows and he rested his gaze upon his precious girls. How he missed touching them whenever he felt like it. Encouraged by their laughter and interest, he reached over, snagged Bonny's curly blond head and gave her cheek a sound smack. The child giggled and kissed him back.

And then it was her mother's turn. . . .

Molding his hands around her fragile jawbone, Jared gently eased her over the length of his body. With slow, deliberate care he kissed her thoroughly. Slipping his tongue between her lips, he probed the moist velvet of her mouth. With a soft breathy moan she melted over him, like a stick of butter in the blazing sunshine.

The kiss lasted only a few seconds and to all appearances was a playful exchange. But the two of them knew differently. They'd tasted liquid lightning.

Kate shifted on the lawn awkwardly, peering at Bonny's form as it slipped into the playhouse. "Where is this coming from, Sam?" she whispered. "I mean, we never felt . . ." The awe in her voice embarrassed her a little. She didn't mean to insult him. And to the contrary, he seemed completely satisfied.

"Enjoy the ride, Kate. Sit back and let it happen."

She began to rise, first to her knees, then to her feet. "But it seems so soon. Too soon."

"But surely not wrong?" he challenged.

"No, no." She gazed down at her knotted fingers. "Only too right."

"Then we have nothing to lose."

The man had a point. Kate felt she'd lost just about everything. And for the first time in a long while, she was swelling with a wondrous long-forgotten feeling, hope.

BY NOONTIME the temperature had jumped a good fifteen degrees to seventy-five. Jared had stripped off his denim shirt long ago, and was beginning to find even his T-shirt damp from exertion.

He stood back to admire the playhouse. With press board on the roof and white siding, it was really shaping up. He flexed his large tanned hands, his eyes straying to his well-developed triceps as they bunched. Sam's added height and weight were useful, not to mention a lot of fun. The wiry frame Jared had been born with was fine, and he'd always been fit. But Sam...well, the guy had sculpted his body to bronze statue perfection. He couldn't imagine spending hours in the gym the way Sam had, but surely with a fitness regimen, including Kate's healthy meals, he could maintain it to his satisfaction.

"Here you go, Uncle Sam." A panting Bonny nudged into his hip as she came to an abrupt stop. "Here's Daddy's sunglasses. They were in the top drawer, just like you said."

"Thanks, Bonny bunny." He set the aviator style frames on his nose, and gazed around the expansive yard, satisfied with the clarity of the amber lenses. Sam had collected two dozen pairs of junky shades, which were stuffed everywhere in the apartment and the office. His excuse had been that he was always losing them, or crushing them beneath his feet or rear end. Now that Jared had lived in his shoes—literally—for a while, he was convinced that Sam had been a plain, unadulterated junk hound. Glasses hadn't been his only vice. Jared had unearthed as many cheap watches and razors, as well as an entire collection of video cassettes featuring—who'd have ever guessed—television shows from their boyhood. Poor Sam had been stuck in a time warp, dating back to the happy days he'd spent with Jared's folks. No wonder he'd battled Kate for Jared's attention. No wonder he'd never married.

Oh, how Jared longed for all his own stuff back! He couldn't wait for the day when he and Kate could sort through Sam's stockpile and send the bulk of it to charity.

Bonny was tugging at his beltloop for attention. She'd started it when she was knee high and he'd always loved it. Cupping her soft chin in his hand, he asked her what she wanted.

"How'd you know I'm Bonny bunny? Only my daddy calls me that."

Jared rubbed his lips together. He'd been so comfortable, he'd forgotten himself.

"And how'd you know where those sunglasses were?"

"Guess I'm just super smart," he said with chuckle.

"I think I love you, Uncle Sammy," she confided merrily, her china blue eyes huge. "I always liked you. But now I probably love you."

"I love you for sure, baby." He squeezed her chin a little tighter. He had to get this right! He couldn't bear another loss. But the nagging feeling that he could blow it with Kate with the wrong move or word, forever gnawed deep inside him.

"What's the deal out here?" Kate moved across the lawn to join them, looking fresh and radiant in green pencil-slim slacks and a soft beige sweater. Her hair, freshly styled above her shoulders, had a blue-black sheen.

Jared turned his wrist and glanced down at one of Sam's gold-tone watches. Earlier Kate had told him of the meeting at the school, but then it had seemed so far away.

"You goin' already?" Bonny piped up in complaint.

"Yeah," Jared chimed in. "Are ya?"

Kate laughed at their bleak expressions. "Have to get used to the old routine again. And this is only the beginning."

"Mommy, I don't want Aunt Martha to come over," Bonny blurted with a stomp of her tennis shoe. "Sam can stay with me instead."

"Oh, honey, Martha's due any minute." She looked at a loss. "You adore her."

"'Course I do. She's fine for baking and stuff, but she can't run around, hammer nails, or twirl me in the air."

"Yes, I saw Sam doing that through the window and he's really not supposed to. Not until he's mended."

Bonny stuck her lower lip out far enough to easily shelve a penny. "But he twirled you first."

"Yeah, Mom," Jared purred. "Just trying to be fair."

Kate huffed in halfhearted disgust. "You two!"

Jared cleared his throat as he spotted Martha and Walter coming around the side of garage. "They're here."

"Behave, Bonita Katherine Reed," Kate said firmly, then whirled around with a dazzling smile and welcoming arms open wide.

"The professional sitters!"

The retired couple moved across the lawn in perfect sync with cheery waves. The schoolteacher carrying her wicker knitting bag, and the cop holding a sportsman's magazine were a matched, inseparable set with their loose budgetwise clothing and their clipped gray hair.

Kate embraced them excitedly, full of good-humored chatter. As selfish as Jared was about wanting time with his daughter, he knew it was only fair that the Helsers have their share as always.

"Didn't know you'd be coming today, Walter," Kate told him, suddenly looking a lot like Bonny as her face crumpled in a pout. "Thought you might be checking into . . . official things."

"I'm doing what I can," Walter assured her, his fleshy face pinched in frustration. "Just have been finding doors tougher to open now that I've turned in my badge."

Jared made a grunting sound, thinking how unimportant Walter was making being relegated to an outsider's position at the station sound in front of Kate. He'd been ready to explode over it at Shooter's.

Walter turned to him then, his bushy brows joined to form one long bottle-cleaner bristle. "So what are you doing here, Romeo?"

"Man's work," he joked in a deep tone.

Walter's watery blue eyes glinted. "Didn't know you were handy—with tools."

Jared pushed his sunglasses up higher on his nose, stalling, thinking. This handyman role was a bit of a stretch for Sam, true. But he'd always been ready to try new things. Jared reminded himself that a big part of this charade was attitude. Sam had had a lazy arrogance about him. It instilled confidence and made people careful about challenging him.

Kate intervened before he could speak. "I deeply appreciate his help, Walt. It would've cost a lot to hire somebody. And the budget is tight."

Martha clicked her tongue, signaling her agreement. "Know just what you mean, Kate. We've been saving up our money for a few years, so we can buy a secondhand trailer and tour the country."

"Ah, Marthy," Walter wheezed.

"We're goin', Walter Helser! I've spent a lifetime seeing everything through textbooks and you've spent a lifetime with thugs. We're hitting the road next week and that's final!"

Jared was surprised. He'd had no idea that the Helsers had such elaborate plans. And by the sullen expression on Kate, it appeared she hadn't either. How she'd miss them!

Kate and Jared soon made their goodbyes, and moved toward the house. He longed to put his arm around Kate's shoulders in a gesture of reassurance, but didn't dare. The garage door was still open and the back service door stood ajar. Walter would be watching Sam's every move like an anxious papa. They did pause together in the driveway, though, between the van and the sedan, as they had so many times as man and wife.

"Thanks for coming, Sam."

"I could've stayed with Bonny today," he blurted. "Would've gladly."

Her eyes twinkled. "I can see that. And believe me, another ally is just what I need."

He did curve his arm around her shoulders then, press his lips to her temple. "You're safe, Kate. I promise. Especially here at home. The security system in this house is top notch."

"But the investigation troubles me. I have the awful feeling that we're caught between the crooks and cops."

"So it appears," he admitted. "But Valley View Investigations is in the clear. We were just doing our job, right up till the accident. Dennis Edgerton needs to broaden his focus, that's all. Understand that we are the losers in this situation."

She rested her chin on his chest, with a soft sigh. "Seems like people just keep bailing out on me. First Jared, now the Helsers."

"You're not alone though. You have plenty of friends and colleagues around you." His voice quavered a bit. Never had he seen his wife so vulnerable.

He turned to humor to ease the tension. "You won't be losing me, that's for sure. The idea of touring the country in a mobile home leaves me with a queasy stomach. As does the thought of all those truck stop meals."

Kate lifted her chin with a self-conscious look. "Don't mean to sound like such a wimp, really."

"Admitting a need or a feeling isn't wimpy at all," he said huskily, tracing his finger along the neck of her sweater. "And . . . I happen to believe I need you right now a lot more than you need me."

Kate's eyes crinkled at the corners as she scrutinized him. "I never could tell when you're lying, Sam."

"Good."

"Good?" she repeated, puzzled.

"A guy's gotta have at least one self-defense weapon in his corner." He touched her face and with a crooked smile moved to open the door of the van for her. She stepped up into the driver's seat and inserted the key in the ignition. He put his hand over hers on the wheel. "Drive carefully."

"Yes, sure." Her voice was breathless, her face glowing with anticipation.

She wanted him to kiss her. He could sense it clear down to his toes. "Did you know Walter's watching us?" he asked mildly.

"No!" she exclaimed, resisting the temptation to look through the windshield. "The protective old coot."

He squeezed her hand a little harder. It was so hard to let go! "We could meet later."

"But I— Bonny is—" She groped for words, her face flushed.

"It's okay. We both have business to take care of."

He watched her back out of the driveway and disappear down the curving street. Walter had miraculously disappeared as she did. After a moment Jared could see his stout khaki-clad figure easing into the playhouse after Bonny.

It was petty perhaps, but Jared was beginning to look forward to Walter's road trip. The cranky fossil needed some new interests. Leave it to practical Martha to steer the bull in the right direction.

8

JARED HAD ALL but forgotten about Ida Turner's Thursday visits to Sam's place. He'd returned to his apartment after a trip to the hardware store to find the diligent housekeeper running a vacuum cleaner over the worn tan carpeting in the living room. Sam might have been a sucker for a pretty face, but he'd done a superb job of looking beyond surface beauty when hiring Ida. A no-frills woman in her fifties, with a pear shape body and salt-and-pepper hair piled high on her head, she was the perfect house mother for this one-man fraternity.

Jared shifted the grocery sacks full of playhouse supplies in his arms, as he fumbled to turn the doorknob and ease inside without a spill. At the top of one of the sacks sat something for the apartment, a replacement dead bolt for the door. Luckily, it had only two keys, which would make it easier to avoid offering Ida one. It was hard to envision the cleaner, who had a passel of children and was married to a respected auto mechanic, as a suspect. But the detective in him weighed Ida's circumstances with objectivity. With her brood, money would presumably be in short supply on occasion. Though not the type to rob a museum, she might have been bribed to spy on Sam by someone who wished to harm him.

This seemed like a fine opportunity to have a chat with her, get some impressions. Not wishing to start things off with a scare, he waited until she turned the vacuum sideways, and spotted him on her own.

Despite his good intentions, she gasped in shock. "My ears and whiskers, Sam Stone!" She quickly shut off the upright machine, then stared at him blankly, her chest heaving beneath a jade velour top.

Jared was sheepish. "Tried not to startle you."

"A woman raising five kids gets accustomed to it, I suppose." Recovering her composure, she marched up to give him a hug. "Good to see you back, in one piece." She gave his cheek a perfunctory pat, as she might one of her own brood, then stepped back to inspect him. "You don't look too bad really, aside from the bruises on your forehead. You still in a lot of pain?"

He smiled warmly over her concern. "It comes and goes."

She set a hand on her padded hip, curious as he dug into his sack. "Yahoo!" she rejoiced. "A brand new lock! Maybe that knock on the noggin' did you some good after all."

His eyes narrowed. "What do you mean?"

"You know what I mean." She wagged a finger at him. "How many times have I told you to secure this place? World ain't safe. I shudder to think of all the keys you got floating around Denver proper, not to mention the outlying areas. And somebody like you, who sees the seedier side all the time, knows better."

Jared inwardly conceded that Sam, like everyone else, had had his contradictions in personality. For instance, he thought it rude to ask an old lover to return a key. He'd track a thug through a dark alley, but was a coward with a huffy playmate.

"Well, you'll be happy to know I plan to play it safer in the future," he announced with good humor, bending to lean the bags against the coffee table. "We're starting off with a clean slate. No uninvited visitors." He straightened again, affecting a regretful look. "I'm afraid I can't give you a key just now. Thought I'd give the only spare to Kate Reed. She's the closest thing I have to family."

Ida beamed with approval. "Spoke to her at the hospital and was very impressed. Say, did you go through some kind of complete rebirth in that coma?" She added apologetically. "What I mean to say . . . I've never seen this place so neat—you even made your bed."

Jared laughed, squeezing her shoulders as he'd seen Sam do. "Guess you could say so." Keeping his sinewy arm clamped around her, he led her to the sofa. "There are a few things I'd like to discuss with you right now, if you have a minute?"

Ida sat beside him, splaying her work worn hands on her thighs. "Okay. Shoot."

"First of all," Jared began awkwardly, "I'm afraid I can't remember everything—details, I mean. For instance, how much do I owe you in wages?"

"Let me see . . ." Ida rocked on the cushions. "We're moving into the end of August, so I figure you owe me about five hundred dollars."

"That much!"

She reared back, and said defensively, "Well, sure. Forty bucks a week. Twelve weeks counting this one."

Jared grimaced. Damn that Sam. He'd owed her even before the crash. How could he have let that slide? No question though, he could be careless with those who cared for him most.

Ida assumed his scowl was aimed at her. "Now, it really would be four hundred eighty, technically speaking. And those weeks you were laid up, why the cleaning was light. I'm sure we could come to some sort of compromise."

"No, no, Ida. Fair is fair. I'm very grateful you didn't fill my slot with another job."

"We had a family meeting about it, just after the crash," she admitted. "Me, Barney and the kids took a vote and everybody was in favor of having mercy on you. Barney pointed out that this is my easiest job, being just the one bathroom, and it'd be a shame to lose it. And over the years you've managed to charm all the kids, when you stopped by at dinnertime and told them tales of derring-do. They're divided between crushes and hero worship, think you can do no wrong!"

Jared could feel his face redden over Sam's obvious mooching. But it would be like him to gravitate to their family situation. He so loved gleaning comfort without sticking his neck out emotionally. "In any case, I'm sorry about the delay," he finally said. "Guess I lost track of time. With the kids, expenses must be tight."

"They are," she conceded. "And I appreciate your finally noticing."

It was a backhanded compliment, but again, Jared could only do damage control. He leaned forward and extracted his wallet from his back pocket. It wasn't his way to carry a lot of cash around, but the trip to the bank to check into Sam's accounts had been uncomfortable, with the question of signature and all, so he'd taken out quite a sum. It was hidden in different parts of his wallet at the moment. Ida's blue eyes widened as he extracted six one hundred dollar bills and a fifty from the main compartment.

"Here you go, Ida."

She folded the cash and pushed it into her pants' pocket. "Thank you so much! Now I'm owing you."

"Not at all. Not when you consider interest, loyalty and the groceries you bought."

"Not sure I did enough now!"

"I'd like to put your head to work for a few minutes more," he proposed. "Then I'll be more than satisfied." She was eager to oblige, so he went on to explain that somebody had caused the accident by fiddling with his brakes. She listened, her milky face losing even its faint peachy hues. If her distress was an act, it was a terrific job. "Under the circumstances, I'm not comfortable with your being here alone, without my protection. It slipped my mind to cancel you today and I'm sorry."

"Oh, yes, I see," she said slowly. "Though I'd feel perfectly safe once you have that in place," she said, gesturing to the new dead bolt resting at the top of the bag. "It's bound to keep out any pests."

"That leads me to my next question, Ida. Who's been hanging around since the accident? Anybody in particular been a pest?"

"Gretchen, of course," she replied promptly and snappily. "She's the only one I know of. You see, I popped in here frequently while you were laid up, kept close tabs on things."

"That was very, very kind."

A light color touched her cheeks at his praise. "Well, it wasn't that big a deal. I watered the few plants you haven't killed off, used the lights at different times, tried to make the place seem lived in. Kids helped out. Mickey even took over sometimes," she added proudly. "He's nineteen now, you know, almost twenty. Busy as a bee at his father's garage this summer, repairing cars, but more than glad to stop in here to use your television and telephone, make a little noise for appearances."

Wow-wee, Jared thought. Takes a real trooper to change channels and yak it up! But this slant on Ida's eldest son was no surprise. Sam had spoken of Mickey often enough. On stakeouts, for instance, they'd had fun reading into Ida's glowing reports for a clearer picture of him. He seemed like a decent kid, no drug habit or destructive tendencies. But he had had some minor brushes with the law for reckless driving and underage drinking. Jared was sure the kid hadn't done a minute of real work around the apartment.

Deep creases appeared between Ida's thick brows. "To tell you the truth, I grew sorry Mickey ever set foot in this place. After that viper Gretchen got her claws into him!"

"How, Ida?" His tone was sharper than he'd intended, but he wasn't prepared for this kind of bombshell!

"It happened last week," she went on with mounting steam. "What I've pieced together is that she saw the lights on up here and assumed you'd been released from the hospital. Crept inside—with her key—like a tigress in heat!"

"How could she make such a mistake?" Jared objected, remembering that, according to Sam, all her kids were on the fair side.

"Mickey was straightening things in your refrigerator when it happened, I understand. You know, leaning over," she clarified in a low significant tone.

Jared interpreted the message. Mickey was making a snack for himself and one butt resembled another in that dimly lit kitchen.

"Anyway, she snuck up on him and well, sort of goosed him I guess!" Her mouth was pinched in a thin line, and she appeared a trifle embarrassed. "He's never been touched that way before, which made it all the more disturbing."

Yeah, right. Jared's expression must have registered his doubt because Ida's voice grew shrill.

"It's true. He sort of yelped. Then made a production of letting her know that I was here. I can tell you I barreled out of the bedroom with your big flashlight in my hand!"

Jared paused to think. A red-blooded teenage male upset because the well-stacked Gretchen grabbed his crotch? It didn't wash. It made more sense to assume that Mickey was warning Gretchen that Ida was there, didn't it?

"If you don't believe me, you can ask him yourself," Ida suggested. "Mickey!"

He was here now? Jared wondered with a start. Sure enough, the bathroom door creaked open and a strapping young buck in tattered jeans and a Green Day T-shirt loped into sight.

"Hey, Sam." The teenager raked some straw-colored hair out of his eyes, then folded his beefy arms over his chest in a defensive gesture.

"We were just talking about Gretchen," Ida prompted.

"Yeah?" Mickey made a clumsy attempt at boyish innocence, but the lust in his eyes was unmistakable.

Jared gritted his teeth. "So you've met her," he said dryly.

"Yeah, Sam. I've been hangin' out here while you were in the hospital. You know, to make the place look lived in."

Living in Sam's place seemed like a better bet, Jared thought.

"I was telling Sam how Gretchen pops in whenever she likes," Ida inserted. "How she, uh, confronted you at the refrigerator."

Fear flashed in the boy's eyes, but he kept a steady smile. "Oh, that was nothin', Sam. No reason to be jealous."

"I can handle it," Jared assured him solemnly.

"Sam understands that she made a mistake when she attacked you," Ida hastened to clarify. "That you were completely innocent."

Mickey's head bobbed in agreement, but the hunger in his young face was blatant. He moistened his thick lips, and seemed on the verge of drooling. Jared was suddenly sure he'd sampled all of Gretchen's abundant charms.

So what did it mean? Presumably they'd met here at the apartment along the way and clicked. Gretchen's motives were the important ones, of course. She would be controlling the show. Was she simply satisfying her sexual appetites, or steering Mickey around by the crotch for other reasons?

Jared didn't like the dark answer that popped into his mind. Maybe she'd met Mickey before the accident, and had lured him into the scheme to end Sam's dogged search for the stolen jewelry. The car accident had been staged by someone who knew something about cars. Mickey no doubt had learned a few tricks helping out at his father's garage and could conceivably tamper with a brakeline.

Ida was scowling now, trying to read her employer's mind. "Do you see where I'm going with this, Sam? Why I've spoken out? If I'm stepping out of line it's only because I care, because we've been friends for so long." She inhaled, then rushed on with new intensity. "This Gretchen is bad news for all of us, no two ways about it."

"You may have a point," he agreed, appearing grateful.

Ida sighed with relief. "The sooner she's gone, the better."

Jared had the feeling that Ida's problems with Gretchen were only beginning, but kept silent. Mickey was the one who was hooked, and they wouldn't need Sam's apartment to get together.

"It won't be easy to convince her," Ida said, giving his shoulder a motherly pat. "Why, she was even here again today—"

"Today?" Jared exclaimed. "Why?"

"Came for some of her panties she said. Had to have the black ones that fit under her leotards she said," Ida replied caustically.

A bark of laughter climbed his throat as he imagined the scene. He swallowed fast and hard. "You doubt it?"

"Well, that kind doesn't wear panties under leotards, do they? Anyway, I dogged her the whole time, never let her out of my sight. She finally grabbed the undies and stormed out."

"Wonder what she really wanted."

Ida shifted closer on the couch and lowered her voice. "To surprise you in bed, is my guess. It was early. She let herself in and crept right to the bedroom, added a gob of lipstick, unbuttoned her blouse—I watched the whole thing from the kitchen." Ida grinned wickedly. "You should have seen her face when I snuck up on her with an overripe cucumber. Paid her back for my Mickey!"

Jared glanced at Mickey, slumped against the door-jamb, a sour expression on his face. Either he didn't take to Gretchen's fickle libido, or hated to see a cucumber go to waste. "Maybe you should be my bodyguard, Ida," he suggested with a wink.

She chortled. "Had plenty of experience with my Barney, Sam. You wouldn't believe what women would do for a simple lube job in this city."

"What, Ma?" Mickey demanded eagerly, prowling closer. "What would they do?"

"Never you mind, son." Ida waved him away. "Now shoo on out of here. You're supposed to be registering over at the junior college today."

Mickey's reluctance was obvious as he shuffled slowly across the room, grabbed a zippered sweatshirt off the back of Sam's easy chair and reached down for a candy bar wedged in the cushion. He shut the door with more force than was necessary.

Ida cringed, but Jared pretended not to notice. "So is there anything else you'd like to tell me, Ida? Anything that happened around here that seemed a little strange?"

Ida rubbed her forefinger over her chin. "Could be. I know there was the one time, last Friday, the night before your release."

Jared curled his fingers, trying not to betray his excitement. "Tell me about it."

"I made my weekly call to the hospital, spoke to that nice Dr. Glenbrook and found out that you were due home. Barney suggested I set out for the grocery store, buy some fresh things for you. He meant junk food, but I proceeded on a healthier mission. This place was shining from the day before, so I stocked the cupboards and left. Then I went home to do my own chores. Well, later on, after dinner, I got to thinking how much you like my pound cake. We'd had it for dessert and I'd made plenty. So I jumped in my car and brought it over."

"It was delicious," Jared broke in gratefully, remembering that it was the only thing that had appealed to him after Kate and Bonny had left him on his own to dwell on the divorce bombshell.

She smiled. "Anyway, it may be foolish, Sam, but when I came back I had the feeling that things had been moved around a little." She gestured to the small drop-front desk near the front door. "It was all very subtle. Appeared to me your bills and pen were set at a different angle. The desk chair seemed a bit off kilter, like somebody had maybe sat there and not quite aligned it with the dents already in the carpet. Course this carpet is so bare it doesn't dent much."

"Anything else?"

She surprised him by continuing. "I could've sworn your tree lamp was closer to the easy chair, that the cushions in this sofa had been fussed with." She added apologetically, "Could be my imagination, my own cluttered mind playing tricks. I'm never that observant at home, and so accustomed to things being tossed around every which way."

"With five kids, that's natural," Jared said absently, wondering how many people had contacted Thomas Glenbrook ahead of time to learn of his release. He was convinced somebody had been here for a reason, and had timed it carefully.

Ida rose and moved over to the vacuum. "Anything else? I really should be heading back to that tossed home of mine."

Jared jumped to his feet. "Go on, Ida. And thanks."

"So, what about next week?"

"I'll call you."

"Fair enough." She looked around as she steered the vacuum toward the front closet. "The way things were today, you might want to consider having me half as often anyhow."

"Think that would be enough?"

She turned around and gave him a wink. "Why, sure. If cleanliness is next to godliness, I'd say you've been to heaven and back on feather duster wings!"

JARED INSTALLED his new door lock, then decided to indulge in a hot shower. Spending time in the confines of the steamy stall was gloriously relaxing, a reminder of how easily he tired these days. He grew so groggy that he even stumbled a little as he stepped out onto the round fringed rug on the tiled floor. He doggedly wiped down his wet body, chastizing himself for not being more careful of his health. Dr. Glenbrook had cautioned him to start out slowly.

But, dammit, there was so much to do! He stalked down the short hallway in his T-shirt and briefs, frustrated by his lack of energy. Did he have a real excuse not to rest? Eve was making a long day of it at the office, typing reports on the legwork they'd been doing. He'd told her he'd try to get there before the end of the day. How it angered him that his body couldn't keep pace with his ticking brain.

He crashed in the easy chair vacated by Mickey, and reached for the remote control on the end table at his elbow. He aimed the remote at the television, and brought a talk show to life on the screen. The show's guests were in the midst of an intense argument concerning the custody of a canary, their voices shrill with outrage. It was campy and Jared was amused, but he shut his eyes against the display to concentrate on his own troubles.

The Turners and Gretchen.... The tangle was so unexpected, and certainly complicated what was already a puzzling investigation. He was ninety percent sure Ida was on the level. But that son of hers, with his automotive background, couldn't be dismissed. And where did Gretchen fit in? Was she just as she seemed? A sex-starved predator moving from one man to another, with no scruples about seducing teenagers? Or was her every move contrived, from her timely appearance in Sam's life, to her interest in the mechanic's son, to her persistence in recharging her affair with Sam? With these concerns tumbling through his mind, he drifted off to sleep.

When Jared opened his eyes again, the room was dark. The television was flickering with an evening news program. Something had awakened him, but what? He listened, but heard nothing above the newscaster. He moved his head from side to side on the easy chair's nubby upholstery with an inward groan. Could it be his new lock was already cracked? Did he have an intruder to contend with?

He sat still, alert and waiting. Quiet moments passed without a sound. He was soon satisfied that the place was empty.

What had awakened him? Maybe it was an internal clock, nudging him into work. But he really didn't want to go in anymore. And Eve would most likely be gone by now herself. Anything important could wait till tomorrow. Settling back, he allowed his eyes to drift closed again.

He began to wind back down in stages, willing his heart rate to slow, his muscles to relax. He remained in a groggy state just short of sleep for quite some time, but no matter how hard he tried, he couldn't seem to nod off. A very annoying static was humming through the center of his brain, with a very clear message.

Like it or not, he had the undeniable urge to go to the office.

VALLEY VIEW Investigations was apparently still open for business when he arrived at ten past seven. The outside door was unlocked and the lights were on. There was no sign of Eve, however; the reception desk was empty. The connecting door to the inner office was closed, but a light from inside was casting a greenish glow on the frosted glass panel. To his chagrin, there was also a familiar musty smell pervading the room.

He strode over and whisked open the connecting door. The lamp glowing was the one on Sam's desk, and beside it stood a tall white vase with a single rose.

"You're late," a feminine voice said accusingly.

With a click, the twin lamp on Jared's desk came to life. Just as he'd suspected, there sat Eve with her burning incense pot centered on the desktop.

She glared at him through clouds of pungent smoke. "I've been calling you for two hours!"

"Through meditation?" He smiled mockingly. "Why didn't you pick up the telephone like most folk?"

"Well, it was sort of an experiment," she admitted.

"Sorry it failed."

She lifted a finger in triumph. "Ah, but it didn't. You came."

He crossed the room to crack open a window. "What's so urgent?"

"Nothing. Anymore."

"Eve . . ." He trailed off threateningly.

"Well, it all started with Kate's phone call."

"She okay?" He spun back around on his heel.

"Sure. She phoned to see how things were going, fished to see if you were around."

"And?"

"I told her you were liable to stop by. She came over—with the rose—and it seemed like the perfect opportunity to do one my experiments, see? Have to keep the psychic muscles in shape."

"Cut to the chase."

She turned her head away from his glare. "I sent you a suggestion to join us."

"Wish you'd dialed direct," he said flatly, picking up the vase on the opposite desk.

"I did, eventually, but you must have been on your way, cause I got no answer. Kate said it was no big deal."

His heart sank like a lead balloon. Kate was reaching out with the kind of spontaneous gesture they'd talked about and he hadn't been here. How could he have been so dense?

"So what took you so long?"

"I was tired, tried to ignore the impulse." He sank into the chair opposite his new partner, holding the rose in front of him like a prized trophy.

"If you need someone to confide in . . ."

"You know somebody?" he joked.

"Very funny." With a sweep of her hand she urged more of the smoke in his direction. "Take some of this!"

He stared at the flower with lovesick eyes. "Maybe I should call her."

"Please don't. She was kind of embarrassed by the whole attempt."

"But I feel cheated. She came over here to tell me about her afternoon, I just know it."

"Well, it sounded like boring stuff to me."

"She discussed it with you?" he demanded incredulously.

"I was all she had. I got the whole spiel, about all the teachers and the things they said and did."

Oh, how he missed those pre-Labor Day stories. Year after year, they'd cuddled in bed to discuss all the characters at the school. Apparently the ritual still meant something; she'd turned to Sam as a stand-in listener. "Go on, then," he directed, his voice warming.

Eve gawked across the aisle. "Huh?"

"Tell me the stories."

"They're a snooze!"

"It's all in the ears of the listener." He sat up straighter, and set the vase on the desk with a thump. "You wrecked this whole set-up with your hocus-pocus and it's only right you make it up to me."

Eve, muttering ungraciously, threw another stick of incense into the pot just to be obstinate. "I could start with the second grade teacher, Miss Baumgarten, obsessive paper collector and tile art expert."

Jared waved extravagantly. "Fire when ready."

9

THE RING of the telephone woke Jared the following morning. He struggled to sit up, thinking how simple it would've been for Eve to contact him this way last night. Rings he heard right away, rings he responded to.

He groped for the telephone on the nightstand. It was a one-piece job, shaped like a tennis shoe; a perk from one of the girlie magazines stowed under the bed, if memory served him right. There wasn't much that Sam hadn't shared with him, tedious details such as the brand of hair spritzer he used and where he bought his socks.

If only he'd told him about the damn ruby ring ahead of time!

He fumbled with the awkward phone, looking for the connector button in the dark room. "Hello? Hello?"

"Sam! It's Kate."

"Kate." He heard terror in her voice and instantly sat up straight. She'd sounded like this only a few times during their marriage: once when her father had gone on a drunken rampage and another time when Bonny had cut her head at nursery school.

"Oh, Sam—" Her voice broke off.

"Tell me what's the matter," he prodded, straining to keep his voice calm. But it was tough to keep control.

He didn't belong here, miles away! "Something about Bonny?" he forced himself to ask.

"No," she blurted out, her voice gaining strength. "Walter just called. Wanted to prepare me for the police. Dennis Edgerton's secured a search warrant and will be here within the hour."

"That's nuts!" Jared's anger, expressed in Sam's booming baritone, was nothing short of a nitro blast.

"It doesn't make any sense," she said tearfully. "Jared didn't do anything wrong. He was straight as an arrow."

"I damn well know it!" Jared bared his teeth, and flicked the covers off his powerful thighs.

"What should I do?"

"Cooperate, Kate. But don't make any statements. Above all, don't tell them Walter warned you—"

"Walter's already made that request! He didn't want me to call a soul, not even you."

"Well, he has to cover himself," Jared rationalized. "He took a risk for you."

"He made that very clear."

"Once they arrive, Kate, call the lawyer—your lawyer," he corrected, remembering he no longer shared John Simmons with her. "Demand that somebody from his office get right over there. Oh, and send Bonny to a friend's," he added in rush. "Right away if you can, before they arrive. It'll save her the trauma of seeing things manhandled."

"Yes, yes, good idea."

He gripped the telephone cord tightly, listening to her calling Bonny in the background. "Kate, still there?"

"Yes."

He stood, stretching his stiff limbs, willing them to respond. "They might not want even you in the house."

"Those jerks." She spat the words bitterly.

He swelled with pride. As disturbed as she was at the idea of the search, she didn't want to bail out of the fort. "Don't argue with them, honey. Your behavior will be watched closely. You have nothing to hide and it wouldn't hurt to show it."

"Can you come over?"

Her sweet request pulled his heartstrings taut. "I wish I could. But they'll be thorough. I'll be dealing with them myself in no time flat."

"Oh, that's right." Her tone became apologetic. "Well, good luck."

"Listen, Kate . . ."

"Yeah?"

"It'll be okay."

Jared let her go then, and quickly punched in Eve's number. Fortunately, she sounded wide awake. He explained that there was a crisis, but gave no details, and even before he could ask, she announced she was on her way over to the apartment.

"I LOOKED LIKE a sex-starved idiot, fiddling with your knob out there in the hallway!" Eve bustled into Sam's living room a short while later, holding an outdated apartment key in her hand.

Jared smiled down at the feisty little redhead with fondness. She must've driven sixty through the city to get here this fast. "I changed the locks. Sorry I didn't hear you right off."

"This better be good, Sammy boy." She released a breath that fluffed her bangs and her root beer eyes sparkled challengingly.

"The cops have decided to toss Kate's house, and that means this place, and probably the office are on the list."

Loyal to the core, Eve's annoyance quickly shifted to the authorities. "What's the angle?"

"Dennis Edgerton didn't believe my version of the accident."

"And is bound to be pushing hard because of the promotion Walt told you about." Eve pushed up the sleeves of her baggy black tunic, and moved over to the window to pull back the curtains. "But he'd need just cause to convince a judge to issue a warrant, wouldn't he?"

"Yes. A probable theory on which to base his suspicions."

"Well, put yourself in his place," Eve suggested. "I can't quite get into the establishment mind the way you guys always could. Of course, Jared was best at it," she added goadingly.

"No argument." He began to pace around the cluster of worn furniture, weighing possibilities. "Dennis thinks we have something. Something connected with the museum robbery, presumably."

She nodded. "Has to be it. I'm sure he isn't looking for the tool that sliced the Camaro brakeline."

"No, he thinks he can bury me if he can uncover some evidence." He rubbed the back of his stiff neck. "Seems to me it would be a good idea to start searching for anything that looks incriminating."

"Great idea." Eve gazed around the room. "I'll take over in here. You can have the sultan's nest and we'll rendezvous in the kitchen."

He moved for the hall, but caught Eve's eye as she leaned over to pull the cushions off the sofa. "A lot of people had access to this apartment, you know, Eve," he said quietly.

She rolled her eyes. "Hey, I know that. You're more than suitable for framing. And whoever staged that accident, well . . . it's most likely they'll stop at nothing to bring you down."

Eve's words rang in Jared's ears thirty minutes later as they spread their findings out on the kitchen table: a complete list of the missing Carson Collection and two airline tickets to the Bahamas. Eve had found the stuff taped to the underside of the bottom desk drawer.

Jared tapped the typed sheet of paper with a finger. "This list is the very one Valley View got from the museum. Recognize the linen bond and the seal?"

"Sure. And your mustard stain in the corner. "

"It's obviously mine," he conceded, "lifted from our file cabinet at some point, complete with plenty of fingerprints. Wonder why our man circled some of the pieces, then hid it away with the tickets."

"Makes it appear that you're up to something."

He ran his blunt nail down the paper, images of the jewels flashing in his mind. "All the pieces circled are of lesser value. Wonder if that's significant?"

"The ruby ring is circled," Eve noted.

"I'm sure that fact has significance," he said forcefully.

"And what about these tickets?" Eve slapped the paper airline envelope across her palm.

Jared checked the departure date. "Why, these were seats reserved on a flight in late May, shortly after the accident. It would give the impression that I was going to skip town after that tavern meeting. Along with a companion," he added darkly.

Eve sighed deeply. "Had you died, it would appear that way."

"What does Dennis think I'm up to!"

"If only we had more information about the official theory." Eve clenched the tickets. "It's a shame Walter retired at such an inconvenient time!"

"I couldn't agree more," Jared replied. "I have other sources, but nobody like Walter. If he hadn't called Kate with today's warning, if she hadn't taken mercy on me..."

"Thankfully, we intercepted this stuff in time!" Eve said on an upbeat note. "If only to trip up whoever's trying to frame you."

"I suspect this stuff was planted on Friday, right before my release. Ida was here in the morning and came back evening, and thought that sometime in the afternoon a few things had been moved, especially around the desk."

"Makes sense," Eve said. "Planting it too soon would have been risky. Ida is a thorough cleaner and lots of people had keys."

"So our culprit would have had to be close enough to me to know about how efficient Ida is." The disappointment in his tone was unmistakable.

"And in a position to call Dr. Glenbrook about your condition without arousing suspicion. I happen to know the hospital staff is very careful about releasing that kind of information."

"On the bright side, we have leads to follow. The travel agency who sold the tickets, Dr. Glenbrook's callers, and Mrs. Ginty across the hall. I want to speak to her about that messenger who delivered the ring in the first place. She may have remembered something more," he added, remembering that Eve knew Sam had done so before his death.

The thud of car doors two floors below drew them to the window. Two unmarked police sedans were at the curb. Dennis Edgerton was leading the posse of four as they moved up the sidewalk.

"Guess it's time for me to scoot, sweetie!" Eve chirped confidently. "Somebody has to play detective."

"Yeah." Jared cast Eve a helpless look. He couldn't ask her. But if she offered . . .

Not another word passed between them. Eve scooped up the list, along with the tickets, before whirling out the door.

DENNIS REQUESTED that Sam stay for the search, so Jared calmly obliged, settling into a straight-backed kitchen chair. He'd acted surprised to see them, but had cooperated with just a dash of the irritation that would be expected of Sam.

Naturally, Kate called in the middle of it all. Dennis answered, announced it was her, and handed over the receiver.

"Hi, Kate. Yes, I figured they might have dropped in on you too," he improvised, casting a jaundiced eye at Dennis. "Naturally they didn't find anything at your place. Though perhaps Dennis should have taken some of Jared's old clothes. His wardrobe is getting mighty raggy."

The shorter, plumper man flinched, and gazed down at his brown suit, tight, but brand new and pressed. His head snapped back up like an angry turtle's as Jared hung up the telephone. "Very funny, Stone. We want to see that office of yours, too. Before you go rifle through it."

"Eve will be in and out," Jared told him breezily. "And I'm sure you won't be offended if I call her with the reminder that you have no right to dive into our case files."

Dennis took the phone before he could attempt to dial. "No need. We know better."

Jared stretched out his legs on the dull linoleum and braced his beefy arms behind his head. "From where I'm sitting, you don't know squat."

Dennis leaned over his chair. "So fill me in, Sam."

"I have. Somebody tried to kill me. Somebody who's involved in the museum robbery."

"What kind of cop would I be if I didn't follow the evidence?" He tapped the side of his large nose. "I admit the old sniffer doesn't care for the scent I've picked up. But I can't very well let you get away with a crime just 'cause I like you."

Jared understood Dennis's nose, but he felt like pinching it closed with a hard twist. "If I'm the bad guy, why would somebody cut my brakeline? Huh, Den?"

The detective's eyes narrowed. "Somebody who thought you were getting a little too greedy, maybe."

What did he think Sam had done? "I'm completely innocent, you bullheaded idiot!"

"Flattering a cop can get you in loads of trouble," Dennis cautioned coldly. The men stared each other down for a long agonizing moment, each mirroring the other's anger and disappointment, until the other officers crowded into the kitchen nook.

"Finished?" Dennis inquired crisply.

They rumbled an affirmative. By their unsmiling demeanor, Jared suspected they'd come up empty.

Will Fisher, the youngest and skinniest of the bunch asked if they should put things back in place.

Jared grimaced. What had they torn apart? He stood up slowly, intent on finding out. "Enough of this torture, fellas, I can't sit still for long periods of time right now." Dennis nodded understandingly, allowing him to pass. Stretching his limbs Jared sauntered into the living room and froze. They'd taken Sam's desk apart piece by piece! Which meant that somebody had given them a very specific tip.

But how to respond? In truth, he felt a rush of relief. With Eve's help he'd bypassed arrest! But how would an uninformed victim behave? He settled for a show of outrage and bewilderment.

"You guys need kindling for winter or what?" He whirled around to confront the detective, arms outstretched questioningly.

Will Fisher took the initiative again. "I think I could put that thing back together with some bolts and glue,

Sam. After hours. It's really a nice desk and shouldn't go to waste."

"Let him do it himself," Dennis scoffed, reaching into his slacks for his car keys. "About time he found a safer way to spend his nights."

Jared began to pick up the pieces of maple, and leveled a tapered wooden leg at Dennis as he strode to the door. "Don't do this at the office, Nancy Drew. Whoever suggested that the secret was hidden in this old desk was lying."

Edgerton's mouth pruned. "Yeah, I admit it was an anonymous tip. And don't think I wouldn't like to get my hands on the tipster!"

"Me, too," Jared agreed grimly.

"Why don't you come along and tell me all about it," Dennis suggested graciously, as though extending a dinner invitation. "We can have a nice chat about the whole thing."

Until I slip up. Jared shook his head and felt a rush of pleasure as he thought about his family. "Nope. I'm on my way to a more important carpentry project."

"UNCLE SAMMY!" Bonny came tearing out of the Reed's sprawling ranch-style house the moment he halted the Lumina in the driveway.

"Hey, Bon." Jared wrestled himself out from behind the wheel, and enveloped the child in a bear hug. "Where's your mommy?"

"Inside," Bonny explained, tugging him along by the hand. "She messed up the whole house—all by herself!"

Kate was plumping decorative pillows on the couch in the family room when she heard their voices in the foyer. Sam had come on his own! Presumably the first free moment he had, considering that she'd called him only a scant ninety minutes ago during his own search warrant nightmare. She quickly checked her reflection in the widescreen television then combed her hair with her fingers and smoothed her pale blue sweats. By the time they reached the back of the house she was circling a heavy easy chair turned on its side.

Bonny folded her spindly arms over her chest. "I still don't get why you did this, Mommy. Hide-and-seek?"

"Sort of, I bet," Jared inserted. "Didn't you tell me you lost a ring, Mom, and tore the place apart trying to find it?"

"Yes!" She held up her right hand. "See, Bonny? The pearl one from our trip to California last summer."

Bonny's small mouth sagged. "Why didn't you say that before?"

"Well, you and your daddy picked it out, and I didn't want you to be upset." Kate knew her voice was high and unnatural. But she wasn't much of a liar, even though it was all too necessary in this instance. Bonny couldn't begin to handle, much less understand, the police pawing through everything.

Jared stepped up to help her with the chair. They righted it with good-humored grunts and groans.

"Good thing you came along," Kate murmured behind a sweep of dark lashes. "To, uh, help me right things around here." Her attempt at gaiety was pathetic. It was clear she was about to crack.

Jared turned to Bonny with a grin. "Why don't you go get our tool belts, kiddo?"

"You come to work on my playhouse again?" she asked excitedly, tugging on his belt loop.

Jared ruffled her blond curls. "What else? Now, scoot. Meet me out back."

With whoops of joy, Bonny dashed out of the room.

It was the last thing she intended to do, but the moment Sam's eyes rested on her with undisguised compassion, Kate collapsed against him. "It was so awful! Dreadful!"

"I know it, honey." He pressed her close, aware that her body was trembling like a frightened kitten's. "And a waste of everyone's time."

Kate rested her cheek on his chest, her heart fluttering as she inhaled his scent. Impulsively, she slipped her arms around his middle and molded herself to him. Why in heaven's name did this suddenly seem like the safest haven on earth? "Jared didn't do anything wrong. I know he didn't!"

He basked in her undying faith in him. "Of course he didn't."

"They didn't treat me this way before—" She broke off awkwardly, shrinking in his arms as though trying to break loose. But he hugged her all the more fiercely.

"Before I woke up," he finished in the tense silence. His arms moved across her back, in an effort to relax her. "I welcome your honesty, Kate." He exhaled as she relaxed again, and rested his chin in her hair. "I figure that maybe the police were giving Valley View a break until they heard my version of the story. Dennis Edgerton came to the office Monday with his cards pressed close to his vest. When my version didn't jibe with his theory, it probably triggered all this trouble."

"They tear up your place this way?" she asked in a wobbly voice.

"Worse. My desk is in pieces—literally."

"That seems weird." She lifted her head a fraction with a puzzled frown.

"Well, they had a tip." Gently stroking her hair, he launched into a rundown of what Eve had found in the desk.

"Who would plant those things?"

"Someone intent on destroying me."

"But why?" she asked with a confused cry.

"Damned if I know, honey," he said pensively, the endearment of old slipping out again without notice.

"But it must be somebody close, right?"

"Most backstabs are by people we know," he said dryly.

"Eve has filled me in about Gretchen and the Turners."

He inhaled shakily. Thank heavens he'd only reported Gretchen's attempt to check his mail and steal his answering machine tape. Eve couldn't have kept that bathtub encounter a secret to save her life! It might not bother Kate much now, but when she finally discovered he was her husband, she would be livid over it.

He cleared his throat. "I think Dr. Glenbrook is the man to narrow our list of suspects. Ida, who I trust is innocent, thinks somebody was in my place sometime Friday afternoon. Presumably our intruder knows of her thorough housekeeping habits and therefore waited until the last minute to plant the stuff, for fear that Ida would find them before the police did."

Kate listened intently, automatically accepting his version of events.

His features softened in pleasure despite the grim topic! Her level of trust in him was on a steady climb. She'd soon be ready to hear his real story.

"I hope you're taking precautions at the apartment."

"I did put a new dead bolt on my door. And brought you the spare key," he added, digging into his front denim pocket.

She took the symbol of trust and intimacy with pleasure, amazed at the bonding process between them.

He stroked her cheek with the back of his hand. "You know, I completely forgot to thank you for the rose."

"Oh!" She blushed with a shy smile. "I suppose you figured me out. I was feeling lonely and remembered our discussion about taking action."

"Wish you'd stayed a little longer. I did finally wake up, and go the office."

"I guess I was a little nervous about it all."

He rolled his eyes. "And you began to think about your spur-of-the-moment act, pick it apart, wonder if you should've come."

"Yes, darn you, yes!" She pounded his chest with a rueful look. "I panicked and bolted. Guess I'm an incurable pain."

"Uh-huh. I am deeply pained," Jared responded. "Maybe you could kiss the hurt away."

It took all of his self-control not to smother her with his mouth. He applied a tender, tentative pressure at first to give her a taste, the chance to pull back. But thankfully, she didn't. Like a dream come true, she parted her lips willingly, nudging his wider for a deeper intimacy. He held her in a tight embrace, losing himself in hot softness of her mouth, the feel of her body. Lord, this was what he'd come back for. This was life to him.

For a time they lost themselves in dizzying closeness, making no effort to think anymore.

A knock on glass startled them apart. Bonny was out on the deck, her nose pressed against the sliding door. "I'm waitin' for you, slow pokey."

Kate laughed, a bit relieved over the interruption. She was beginning to like their newfound friendship a little too much. "Better get on to your next customer."

"Yeah." He scanned her length one last time with open appreciation, then moved across the family room toward the sliding door.

"Oh, Sam? You really shouldn't believe everything they say about you."

He paused, swiveling on his heel. "I shouldn't?"

Kate planted her hands on her hips with a saucy smirk. "Heck, no. Ain't nothin' pokey about you at all."

10

KATE MADE A pot roast with all the trimmings for dinner that evening. She fussed around the kitchen in a good humored flurry as if it were a special occasion. "Sit down, Sam. You deserve a break!"

Jared, extremely grateful for the chance at some more of his wife's cooking, took the platter of meat and vegetables from her hands and set it in the center of the table. "The playhouse is looking good, with the siding up," he remarked, tweaking Bonny's nose as he sat beside her.

"You see the green shutters he bought?" Bonny asked Kate. "And the shingles that match!"

"That was way beyond necessity, Sam," she protested.

"So is this meal. Soup and sandwiches would've been fine."

She eyed him shrewdly as she joined them at the table. "Don't lie to me. You're ready to devour everything in sight!"

He certainly was, with her on the top of the list. Their kiss had revved his engine and Jared sensed that Kate had tasted something that appealed to her, as well. Of course he had a secret advantage, knowing exactly how to kiss her, to hold her. What he'd done had worked its magic. She'd spent the remainder of the afternoon testing the elasticity of their new bond with jokes and playful chatter, weaving a web of intimacy around them that no man would wish to escape.

"Everything's delicious," he enthused, digging into his meat and potatoes meal with gusto.

"'Spose I can't have dessert till I clean my room," Bonny grumbled.

Kate started, as though reminded of something disturbing.

"Maybe Mom will make an exception tonight," Jared proposed.

Kate was fiddling with her fork, pushing her slice of meat around in a puddle of gravy.

Jared stiffened. What was the matter with her? Was she upset with him?

She cleared her throat. "Bonny, dear, you have an invitation to a sleepover tonight," she announced brightly. "Forgot to tell you."

Bonny slurped milk from her glass. "Do not."

"It's a surprise. A new surprise. You won't even have time for dessert. I've already wrapped it up for you to take along."

Bonny set her glass down with thump. "I want to play with Uncle Sammy instead."

"Lila Morgan called—"

"Me and Judy Morgan had a fight. She tore my Rockabilly babydoll's dress."

"By accident, I'm sure. You girls have been best friends too long to let a loose stitch come between you."

Bonny's blue eyes narrowed. "She say she's sorry?"

Kate set her fork down, and her voice grew crisp. "I didn't speak to Judy, just her mother. But obviously she must want to make amends."

"Having a sleepover means saying sorry," Jared teased, reaching over to tug her blond curls. He'd always prodded Bonny out of her fussy moods with humor and knew she'd be in capable hands over at the Morgans.

Bonny grew silent, and thoughtful, judging by the pucker in her forehead. Jared tensed along with Kate, waiting for the child's answer.

"But you won't have anything to do if I go away, Sam," she said plaintively.

"Mommy and I will think of something," he promised with a wink, not daring to look at Kate. Did she have something provocative in mind?

Bonny eventually released a huge sigh and bounced up from her chair. "'Spose I could go."

Kate popped up. "I already packed your bag."

Bonny planted a hand on her small hip. "How come? You always say I'm big enough to do that myself."

Jared's brows jumped as he quickly drained his milk. Kate, obviously in no mood for debate, took her daughter firmly by the hand and led her to the foyer.

When Jared caught up with them near the front door, Kate was on her knee, deftly easing Bonny into her white nylon jacket. On a parson's bench near the closet sat a small pink suitcase and a plate of cookies covered with clear plastic wrap.

"The Morgans live just around the bend in the road," Kate told him, rising to her feet again. "It'll only take me a few minutes to take her."

"I'll do it." Jared swiftly reached for his leather jacket, on a hook beside the bench. "I'm supposed to move around, give the legs a workout." With a quick nod, he ushered Bonny out the front door.

Jared delivered Bonny to her friend's, watched their babbling reunion for a few minutes, then took a brisk walk along the curving streets of the neighborhood. As he'd told Kate, he did need the exercise, but he also needed to blow off some steam. He was on the brink of losing all self-control. Making love to his wife was all he could think about tonight. Everything else was blotted out, pushed way back to the darkest corners of his mind.

And it appeared that she'd set up the opportunity. A gift of privacy wrapped up in a huge shiny ribbon. He'd planned to tell her the truth before making a move, but could he resist if she initiated things herself?

"Kate?" Jared called as he eased through the front door fifteen minutes later, but there was no answer. He made his way to the kitchen first, to find it empty. The food was put away, but all the dirty dishes were still scattered about.

He moved through the spacious one-level house, silently, on the alert. Was this some kind of sexy game?

He caught up with Kate in a bedroom. Unfortunately it was Bonny's.

She whirled around at the sound of his footsteps. "Dammit, Sam! You scared me!"

He looked around at the mess. "What's going on here?"

"Can't you tell?" She tossed Bonny's socks into the top drawer of her dresser. "This is courtesy of the Metro police department!"

"They did this?"

"Yes. Bonny mentioning that she had to clean her room reminded me of the sleepover plans I'd made to get rid of her. The lost pearl ring was a good front, but she'd never believe I did this."

"No. You handled it right." A wave of shame washed over him as he inspected the upturned furniture and emptied toyboxes. To think he'd hoped to find her in a filmy negligee! He was getting way ahead of himself.

"After all you've done, I certainly don't expect you to tackle this job, too," she said.

Jared picked up a teddy bear he'd won at a fair last year, and fingered its fuzzy yellow belly. "You want me to leave?"

"Not really." She measured him, her eyes bright and misty. "I simply figured . . . you'd have better things to do."

"No! I don't. Really, I don't." Intent on making his point, he began to align the stuffed animals on their proper shelf. "I want to help you any way I can. You know that."

She nodded. "As long as it's not pity that's keeping you here."

"Pity?" He twisted his tongue around the word as if it were a sour lemon slice. "C'mon!"

She blushed. "Guess I'm thinking too much again."

"Seems I can't leave you alone for a minute!"

Her smile was warm enough to melt a Rocky Mountain glacier. "Guess you can't."

Though he knew where most things belonged, he allowed Kate to direct him. Working together, they soon managed to put the room in order.

Kate smoothed Bonny's white ruffled bedspread as a finishing touch. When she straightened, she bumped squarely into Jared's chest "Oops!" Her fingertips pressed into the light cotton fabric of his shirt, leaving them both with a heightened awareness of the other.

Sam did the only thing he could think of, he bolted out of reach. He paused halfway down the hall with a heaving breath. Damned if he wasn't trapped in an impossible corner with this charade. The idea of making love to Kate was gnawing at his insides. He'd had about all of this friendship stuff he could take.

Kate rushed out after him, only to cause another collision. They bounced apart again with nervous laughter.

"I think I'd better get going," he said, and turned to move down the hall.

She sighed and blocked his path. "Sam, I've been trying to be open with you, and now I feel like you're running away from me."

How very observant of her!

"You can leave if you want to, but I'd like to know what's wrong. When you tracked me to Bonny's room earlier, you looked so taken aback."

He raised his hands and the corners of his mouth. "The shock of the mess—"

"Had nothing to do with it."

He sighed heavily, remembering the rosebud in the vase in his office. That had taken courage. "Okay. I thought maybe you were planning to . . . well, seduce me." He braced himself for the blast as she began to shake her head dazedly. But he had made a vow that he was going to tell as few lies as necessary.

"I am so obvious!" she lamented. "Sorry if I made you uncomfortable, but I've been so lonely, and you've been so warm."

"So I was right?" he demanded in disbelief.

"Oh, this is too awkward. Forget it." She pushed past him self-consciously.

He caught up with her two steps later, and sank his hands into her shoulders. "Oh, Kate." He said her name with a groan of yearning. "That's the biggest compliment I've ever received."

His voice, smooth as French silk, sent red-hot ripples clear through her. She closed her eyes, leaned back against him, and surrendered to the kneading pressure of his hands. Was it so wrong to want to be touched this way, by this man? She couldn't have imagined it before the accident. Sam had often seemed like a walking, talking cliché in his relations with women. But suddenly he was an exciting stranger, possessing all the qualities of her late husband, with an energy that she'd forgotten existed. The kind of dream lover that could make life seem new again.

"I'm here for you," he was crooning close to her ear. "Any way you want." And he meant it. He'd come to realize that he'd take her under any circumstances, no matter who she believed him to be. He wanted her that desperately.

She was like a liquid flame as she leaned into him with tantalizing pressure. He sagged against the wall, bracing her along his length.

For long luxurious moments she lay on top of him, burrowing her softness into his muscled planes with moans of contentment. Suddenly he recalled an encounter much like this one, against a huge oak tree in the park on the Fourth of July, far from the crowd where they'd watched the fireworks display. It had been their first time for sex. It had been quick, hot and furious, with no thought to consequence or commitment.

How encouraging that Kate wanted a repeat of the very same thing.

"Do we know what we're doing, Sam?" she rasped.

"Oh, yeah." He pushed her hair aside, and dipped his mouth to the back of her neck. She shivered against him with needy anticipation. "It'll be all right, I promise."

Kate allowed her body to relax against his, and shivered with pleasure as his fingertips glided down her arms to her waist. His hands were huge as they splayed across her belly, pressed her against his crotch. She gasped slightly as his erection nudged her bottom. Anxious to hear her deepest, sexiest sounds, he dug his fingers into the hard muscle of her abdomen, rotating her hips harder and harder against him in an undulating motion.

The fact that she believed him to be another man was incinerated in the hot volcano building inside him. His passions were a white-hot point of light behind his eyes that made lucid thought an impossibility. Their passions were unfolding in a surreal tailspin. The hallway was like a narrow, secluded tunnel apart from the rest of the world, and it made him bold. He began to explore her body with more deliberate strokes, then peeled off her sweater and discarded her bra to fondle her lush breasts. His touch roamed to her soft jeans, edged inside her waistband, and clenched her tight buttocks.

Kate's soft moans and ragged little whispers were a potent aphrodisiac. Just as his body threatened to shatter, she cried out in a reedy urgency. "Touch me, really touch...me."

Reaching around, he unzipped her pants, shoved denim and lacy nylon to her ankles, over her feet and out of his way. Cupping her feminine mound, he thrust two long fingers into her moist slit. He slipped his other hand in from the rear, invading her fleshy opening with skillful probing. She gave in to the tingling sensations, quivering in fevered pleasure, perspiration beading her brow.

"Now. Now!" she implored throatily, arching her spine for him.

Keeping his trembling hand clamped to her front, he hastily unfastened his own pants. Leaning harder into the wall, he crouched slightly, grasped her by the hipbones and lowered her over his shaft. Gently testing for comfort, he raised and lowered her over him. The fit was slick and comfortable. He forged on, fueled by her cries, gradually picking up tempo until her satiny back was an ivory blur in their swift and fierce coupling.

Orgasm pulsed through her in a ripping spiral, and he gave in to his own mounting tension. She crumpled back against his chest, with a twist and a moan.

Limp and trembling, they eased themselves to the floor.

Kate shifted awkwardly on the carpet, feeling the roughness of the berber on her thighs. Pressing her hands to her cheeks, she found them aflame. It had felt so good to be desired again, comforted again.

Quiet moments slipped by as they each regained composure. When Jared tried to reach for her, Kate made a show of fumbling for her clothes.

"Why not keep them off, Kate," he suggested mildly.

"What?" Her eyes grew round as she wondered what he expected of her. To her surprise, his smile was endearing and guileless.

"It's time I went," he announced. "We need our sleep."

"Yes. I don't think Bonny would understand finding you here in the morning," she apologized, unable to hide her relief. Even after this, he wasn't going to pressure her.

He slowly rose to his feet and readjusted his sagging clothing. "Good night, honey." He bent to touch her cheek then strode toward the front foyer. He took his time slipping into his leather jacket, and glanced back, hoping she might have gotten up to follow him. But to be fair, skipping around the house nude might be more adventure than she was ready for.

He took the front steps on shaky legs. He was just digging into his jacket pockets for the keys when he heard the front door creak open.

Kate had never looked prettier than she did at that moment, standing in the shadows, enveloped in her crimson all-weather coat. Pressed for time, she'd only bothered to cinch it at the waist. "Hold on a minute." She skipped down the steps in her bare feet, and launched herself into his arms.

"What are you doing out here? It was bad enough in your nightie!"

"That was different," she scoffed. "Nobody can see past this coat."

Except for him, he thought with a hard swallow. As she eased her arms around his shoulders, her lapels gaped open, revealing the plump bare breasts he'd so lovingly squeezed in his hands.

"Oh, lord, honey," he croaked. "What are you doing out here?"

"I just wanted to kiss you goodbye," she replied softly. "We didn't do that, you know."

They hadn't kissed at all during their lovemaking. Feeling sheepish, he dipped his head to hers, her mouth offering welcome heat in the cool night. "I should've been more attentive," he apologized. "It all happened so—"

She pressed her fingers to his lips to shush him. "The choice of position was all my doing, Sam. We both know it."

"You won't hear any complaints from me, Kate."

She was flattered by his gusto, but still troubled. "I feel I should explain something before you go home and put the pieces together in a certain way, and make assumptions."

He raked a hand through his tousled black hair, smiling faintly. "I leave the thinking to you, in case you haven't noticed."

"I'm trying to tell you something serious," she whispered with effort. "That I appreciate your being there when I needed . . . needed somebody."

"We both needed," he said quietly.

"Yes, I did notice. But I do feel it's only fair you should know the whole truth. Now. Before any time passes. I'm sorry—"

"Sorry it happened?" he thundered.

"Shush! You've got it wrong."

He reached out for her arms and pulled her close. "Talk some sense here."

Her shoulders sagged, disappearing deeper into the coat. "All right. The thing is, I hope you won't feel taken advantage of. I mean, I did sort of ensnare you in the hallway."

"I was a helpless goner, all right," he said with a chuckle.

She pushed away from him and stomped her bare foot, which was getting mighty chilly. "You're impossible to talk to. I give up."

He snagged her arm. "No, wait. Please. You've made me a happy dope is all."

"All the more reason to listen, Sam. It's only fair you should know," she blurted in a rush. "I wasn't thinking of you during sex. I was pretending you were Jared all the while. Can you ever forgive me?"

He lowered his eyes, hoping to disguise his unbridled joy. So he hadn't been dreaming. She had shouted his true name during climax.

"I just want you to understand that I'm not leading you on," she continued, touching the soft sleeve of his jacket. "Surely you understand how new my loss is. The idea of truly caring for another man this soon would be impossible. Ironically, you're the one who's forcing me to rethink my feelings for Jared, to realize how much I miss him."

"So you realize the divorce idea was all wrong?" he queried hopefully.

"Maybe it was," she admitted. "I don't know. Would it be so wrong if I'm never sure?"

"Yes, it would!" he wanted to shout, but instead said reasonably, "I don't think it would hurt to sort it out."

"All I care about tonight is your state of mind. This can't be too tough, is it? I mean, you've had sex with friends plenty of times, haven't you?"

Countless times, if he counted Kate among his friends.

She grazed his jaw with her knuckles, her eyes widening in hope. "We can go on as we are, can't we?"

"Try and get rid of me."

"See you tomorrow, then?" She immediately saw hesitancy in his face. "Won't I?"

"I have a physical therapy session in the morning, and then I'm going to follow up on some leads." He tapped her nose. "Can't let Dennis have all the fun."

"Let me come with you," she said impulsively.

"It's bound to be pretty routine," he warned.

"You don't know for sure."

"And Bonny?"

"The Morgans will hold on to her for the day. They've done so before."

He couldn't help but be pleased by the offer. "Okay, then. If I don't hear from you, I'll be back here at nine." He dipped down to give her one last peck on the lips, starting the meltdown all over again.

"YOU SEEM in fine shape, Sam," Dr. Glenbrook said as he entered the small hospital cubicle the next morning, and smiled at the handsome couple seated near the door. "And so do you, Mrs. Reed."

"Call me Kate, please," she invited with a trace of laughter. "I feel we know each other so well."

Glenbrook came to a halt, opened the thick file folder holding Sam's medical records, and scanned them through the reading glasses perched on the tip of his long thin nose. "The therapy went well today?"

Jared nodded. His therapist, whom he'd nicknamed Pretzel Twister, had lifted and turned his limbs every which way to loosen up his muscles. All and all, he had to admit it'd been helpful. He was feeling limber and more relaxed.

"Range of motion good," Glenbrook murmured, scanning the top sheet of the file. "Coordination and balance, strength, all good. If you have no concerns, we can say good-bye till next Saturday."

"There is one more thing." Jared went on ask him about his most persistent callers during the last couple of weeks.

Glenbrook flipped through the papers clamped to the left side of the folder. "Ah, yes. Thought I kept track, just as a courtesy. Walter Helser, Gretchen Travers, Eve Kemp, Ida Turner. Oh, yes, her son called a couple of times, too. Don't have his name."

"I know it," Jared assured him.

"Planning some sort of get-together?"

"Possibly. Thanks, doc."

"Keep well."

Jared grinned. "Doing my best."

"WE DIDN'T LEARN much in there, did we?" Kate said as they wove through downtown traffic. "Everybody called."

He shrugged, keeping his eyes on the road. "True, we can't eliminate anyone, but we now know for sure how wide that circle of interested parties is. All in all, I'd say we scored fine."

"Guess I have a lot to learn about how things are done."

He slanted her a smile. "It'll be my pleasure to teach you, teach."

"So what's next?"

"A visit to Sky-Hi Travel, the agency who supplied those airline tickets."

Twenty minutes later Jared swung into a strip mall not far from Sam's apartment. "Sky-Hi Travel, up close."

"Too close for comfort," Kate observed. "Your place is only two blocks away! Somebody really thought of everything."

"Hopefully not everything," he returned briskly.

A woman inside the agency was busy taping photos of exotic places to the glass storefront when they entered. She was impeccably dressed in a jade suit, her brown hair was cut short and her heavy makeup gave her face an expressionless appearance. She greeted them pleasantly. "Good morning!"

"Hello," Jared answered. "What a nice display."

"Thank you. With autumn on the way, people start to think about hot and steamy winter getaways." She clasped her hands together, giving them her complete attention. "Now, how may I help you?"

It was too warm a day for jackets, so Jared had the ticket sleeve in the pocket of his white cotton shirt. He handed them to the woman. "These tickets to the Bahamas were purchased through you and I'd like to track the buyer if possible."

The agent made a clicking sound with her tongue as she examined them. "Far too late for a refund."

"I'm not interested in one," he hastily assured her, flashing her one of Sam's most brilliant smiles.

She shook her head slowly, not responding as he'd hoped. "Just the same, we keep our files confidential. People deserve their privacy."

If Sam could see this, his ego would be in tatters. She had to be a manhater!

Jared started as calm, sensible schoolteacher Kate gave a shrill cry and began to sob. He turned to find her cupping her hands over her eyes.

"What the—"

She pressed her fingers together and slid him a wink. "Don't say a thing, not a thing!" she cautioned.

"I won't," he promised, marching over to the office's grand oak desk for a tissue. His level-headed Kate was actually attempting a scam!

"He could say 'I told you so,'" Kate weepily confided to the agent in a hushed woman-to-woman tone.

"Men do that," the agent agreed, eyeing up the offending male coldly.

"He'd be right this time, I'm afraid." Kate took the tissue and feigned a mighty blow. "He warned me not marry my dreamboat, but I wouldn't listen." She sobbed again. "Now he's run away with someone else and our joint checking ac-counn-nnt!"

"Now, sis." Jared squeezed her shoulders, giving the agent a somber look. "Mom will end up with another migraine if you come home looking like a red-eyed owl again."

"If I come back without some answers, she's liable to collapse completely."

"Mom's mostly upset that you gave up your job after the wedding."

Kate rarely took her eyes off the other woman. "He said he was rich. Said I didn't need to work. Now...now...I don't even have in-surann-nnce."

"We're just looking for justice," Jared said, planting a kiss atop Kate's head.

The agent's eyes hardened and she marched to the desk. "Never have had much use for men," she called over her shoulder in an unnecessary confidence. She sat down at the computer terminal, and her blunt fingers began tapping the keyboard like machine-gun fire. The screen was soon filling with printed information.

"According to this, a man named Sam Stone bought the tickets." She turned to stare at Sam and Kate, who were hovering over the desk. "Is that the name of your dream boy?"

"No, that's not my dreamboat," Kate peeped in disappointment. Not sure how to proceed, she looked at her companion.

"Cash sale?" Jared asked.

"Yes, it was."

"Anything odd about the circumstances?"

The agent paused, tapping her nails on the desktop. "My code is on the transaction, so I sold these tickets myself . . ."

"Anything you can remember would be so helpful," Jared coaxed.

"Well, not many people bring in seventeen hundred in cash," she admitted, creases appearing in the foundation makeup on her forehead. "You know, it seems to me that it was a woman who bought the tickets. Yes," she declared firmly. "I do recall her bringing out that wad of money. Seventeen crisp hundreds. Naturally I scooted them over to the bank to have them authenticated. They were good."

"What did she look like?"

"A kook!"

"What kind of kook?" Kate asked. "Prettier than me? Tell me the truth!"

The agent leaned back in her large cushioned chair. "I truthfully cannot say. She wore a floppy hat, sunglasses, and a coat way too heavy for the May weather. I thought maybe she was eccentric, or sensitive to light."

Jared compressed his lips. Someone with a sensitivity to light wouldn't be off to the Bahamas. But the agent would have understandably been discreet, with so much cash in hand.

"We could call the police," she suggested suddenly, swiveling to the console phone opposite the computer.

"No, no," Jared said slowly, as though weighing the idea. "This is just another dead end."

"You know, I think that Sam Stone worked with my love," Kate said suddenly, scooping up the tickets that would so interest the police. "Let's take a ride over to the Shoe-a-rama and see."

With a gracious thank-you, they retreated.

They were still laughing as they entered the lobby of Sam's apartment building a short while later.

"What would your students have said about that performance?"

"Sneaky seventh graders? They'd have absolutely loved it!"

"I certainly loved it," Jared crooned. Resting her against the mailboxes he kissed her slowly, deeply, until she moaned the way he liked.

She gently eased him away, eventually. "So, what did we get out of that trip?"

He braced his hand over her head. "Backs up the frame theory with amazing strength."

"Kind of an expensive detail, isn't it?"

"Yes." He used his free hand to finger her hair. "Unless the tickets were supposed to be used by two very real fugitives, then weren't because I didn't make the frame airtight by dying."

"Oh!"

"Steady," he said mildly. "No place in this for shaky nerves."

She closed her eyes with a nod. "I know."

"I figure our culprit planned all along to muddy my involvement in the search for the missing jewelry. Had I died in the accident, the cops would've found the ring and the money and without my version would have drawn the obvious conclusion. Why, even the map had disappeared."

"Taken by whoever sliced the brakeline?"

"Probably."

"Certainly a lot more to this job than I ever realized," she marveled with weariness. "It's easier to see why Jared was so consumed with his work. Must be impossible to leave it behind sometimes, during the off hours."

"He always tried though. Never made a secret of how much he enjoyed being a family man."

She seemed to take him at his word. "So, are there any more avenues to cover?"

He raised his index finger. "An easy one that we can take care of here and now."

"MESSENGER?" Mrs. Ginty escorted them into her living room with the aid of her walker. Kate looked around, amazed that this apartment was only a matter of feet away from Sam's bachelor's lair. The decor was a world away, Victorian right down to the doilies on everything and the tweety music of parakeets in the background. "Didn't we discuss this once already, Sam?"

He smiled at the spry old lady, guessing her to be about ninety and weighing the same. "We did, but my memory fails me since the accident."

"Ah, yes, we did talk before the accident." She inspected him through her thick lenses. "How'd you like a nice glass of lukewarm lemon water?"

"Not today, thanks."

"Flushes out those germs."

"Next time."

"But you always have it," she pressed, clearly perplexed.

Jared grinned, envisioning Sam gulping down the citrus concoction to please this lovely senior citizen.

"I'd have to check with my doctor, see if it would affect the drugs I'm taking."

"Very well," she said, surrendering.

Kate sat on one of the plump tapestry chairs, and smiled as a large white cat jumped into her lap. She stroked it gently. "Is there anything you remember about the messenger, Mrs. Ginty?"

The frail old woman leaned on her walker, staring into space as she gathered her thoughts. "'Twas a man. Too rude to remove his cap."

"In uniform?" Jared asked.

"Yes. Like I told you before, dear, there was no name tag on his shirt, no company name on his hat. He was just a rude young man. The sort so common on the street today."

"Young and concealed in a uniform?" Jared repeated thoughtfully.

"Yes, I just said so." She favored Kate with a smile. "Tittles likes to be stroked."

"Lovely cat."

"You staying for dinner, boy?" Mrs. Ginty asked flatly.

Jared's eyes widened. "Excuse me?"

"It's a Saturday, Sam. The family's coming with the Chinese carryout. Are you staying?"

Jared blushed. Another of Sam's stowaway families.

"Of course he'll stay," Kate answered for him.

"But I don't want to stay!" Jared objected as they walked down the street a short while later.

"But you should," said Kate. "She obviously wants you to. Probably was worried sick all the while you were gone."

"I suppose..."

"And Bonny's liable to be tired after the sleepover. I think we'll just make an early night of it."

He heaved a sigh, hooking his thumbs in his belt loops. "Okay. Just so you know, I won't be around tomorrow morning. Eve and I are driving up to Creekside Tavern in Estes Park to speak to the owner."

"Well, Bonny and I have plans of our own, too. Martha and Walter want us to haunt the flea markets with them."

His brows jumped in surprise. "You never cared much for that kind of rummaging, did you?"

"Not really. But they're leaving town next weekend for that extended tour of—I'm quoting Walter now—'these United States of America,' so it's more of a chance to visit than anything else."

He was nonplussed by the news. "Walt actually bought a trailer?"

"A secondhand one from an ad in the newspaper," Kate confirmed. "Guess you never know people, do you?"

Jared shook his head in wonder. "Guess not."

11

THE HIGH ALPINE country of Estes Park was majestic in the bright light of day. Jared could feel Eve's eyes upon him as he steered the Lumina up the narrow winding roads leading to the town proper. The view of the craggy peaks of the Continental Divide, rising into a pure cobalt sky was a breathtaking portrait of nature. He fought to keep these brand new images in his head, rather than the darker ones from his deadly ride with Sam.

The Creekside Tavern was several miles beyond town, past a garish man-made water slide and a couple of souvenir shops. It looked quite charming in the daylight, a cozy log cabin set in a cluster of pines. There were a few big rigs parked at an angle on the left side of the building. Jared wheeled into a spot right in front of the quaint porch.

Eve collected her purse from the floor as he turned off the ignition. "So, we ready?"

He peeled off his sunglasses and set them on the dashboard. "Remember, if he's into law and order we make it appear that we're helping the boys in blue. If Dennis irritated him during questioning, we swing the other way, painting me as the harassed party."

"Gee, I never knew how much fun you guys had in the field."

Jared opened his car door. "In either case, bat those beautiful lashes of yours."

"Isn't fair," Eve griped. "I have to be the vamp, while Kate got to play the frazzled nutcase. Should be the other way around."

His mouth split into a huge grin. "Don't I know it."

Wayne was behind the counter, flipping pancakes on a sizzling griddle. He was just as Jared remembered him, a huge block of a man outfitted in white cafeteria clothes, with a large head squared off by a flattop cut. Jared gestured to the stools closest to the griddle. He and Eve sat down, murmuring to announce their presence.

Wayne whirled around, clutching a spatula in his beefy hand. "Be with ya in a minute." He turned back to the griddle and expertly eased the giant cakes onto a platter. "Coffee, breakfast?" he called out over his shoulder. "Menu's on the wall."

"Something cool, like ice tea," Eve purred. "I'm sizzling inside."

Jared hid a smirk. She was going to play a vampy nutcase. "You remember me, Wayne?" he asked evenly.

"No. You want tea, too?"

"Sure."

He served them, never taking his eyes off Eve. "Think I'd remember you, though."

Eve rubbed her chin with her left hand, to bring attention to her empty ring finger. "Feeling's mutual."

"I was in that car accident back in May," Jared ventured.

"Oh, yeah. You and that blond guy." Wayne tore his eyes from Eve to measure him. "Heard one of you made it."

"Did the police tell you that, Wayne?" Eve asked.

"Uh-huh."

"Ask you a lot of questions?" she queried liltingly. Her hand resting on the counter remained still as he brushed it with his.

"A lot of crap I couldn't answer," he complained to Jared. "What did the two guys do while they were here? Did they talk to anybody? Did I see any money?"

"So did you have any answers for them?"

His small eyes narrowed, almost disappearing in his large face. "You know what I know. I was running the place single-handed. The girls were looking you over. And money? Why, you cheapos didn't even leave a tip."

"Guess we had a lot on our minds." Jared lifted his hip to extract the wallet in his back pants pocket. He peeled three ten dollar bills onto the counter, and edged them under his saucer. "A tip for last time. A tip for this time. And a tip for information. What do you say, Wayne?"

"What are you after?" he asked in bewilderment.

"Facts about that night. What you told the cops, anything else that comes to mind."

"I told them about the extended cab truck that parked next to your car," he reported, straining to be helpful. "Wasn't there long. I remembered it because the man never came in."

"You saw the driver?" Jared asked sharply.

"As he climbed back into the cab."

"Tall or short, fat or thin?"

Wayne shrugged. "Tall, I suppose. Too dark to tell much else."

Jared and Eve exchanged a disappointed look.

"But I wondered, what's he doing back here again, without that woman?"

Eve nearly climbed over the counter in her excitement. "He'd been here before? With a female?"

Wayne beamed under Eve's approving look. "Yeah, recognized the truck. It roared with a fancy engine, but it had a crummy body. Didn't make sense."

"Probably was souped up just for the accident," Jared deduced.

Wayne's interest shifted to Jared. "That driver run you off the road? For real?"

Jared's face was grim. "Yes."

"The cops said it was a brakeline thing."

"So what about the man and woman, Wayne?" Eve persisted. "See them the first time?"

"Just their outlines in the lot. In the dark. It was busy and someone else must have served them. I only noticed them outside because of the sound of the engine, because it was different." His mouth drooped. "'Spose that isn't enough for the dough."

"Sure it is." Jared pushed the bills at him. "And thanks."

"Come on back, little lady," Wayne called after them. "Anytime."

They exited, stepping to the left on the narrow front porch to make way for a family of four.

Eve sighed. "Think you got your money's worth?"

"Certainly. We've got a pattern forming here. Two airline tickets. A couple in the truck. Seems we have a team for sure." He peeled off his leather jacket. "Hold on to this for a sec."

"Why?"

"Just can't bring myself to get behind the wheel without checking the brakeline," he said, extracting his penlight from his shirt pocket.

"Oh, you can't be serious."

His expression remained steady. "We had our backs to the window."

"Wayne didn't!"

Jared lowered his back onto the rough bed of gravel. "You want to bet your life on his observational skills?"

She gulped, hugging his jacket. "Watch your head down there."

With a wry smile he edged underneath the car. He reappeared moments later, looking satisfied. Eve helped him to his feet, brushing the stones off his tan knit shirt. "It all checks out."

"Maybe I should drive us home, hon. I mean, this whole ordeal has to be tough."

His features softened. "Aw, no, Eve. I'm fine."

"At least past the spot where it happened," she pressed.

"You know the spot?" he gasped. "Why didn't you say so on the way up?"

"Thought you knew, thought you were avoiding it."

"No, it's all a blur. One that I probably need to put into focus."

She directed him to the small jut in the road with no trouble. "Had to see it for myself, before they repaired it," she explained. "Sam?" Eve patted his white knuckles on the steering wheel, and gazed down at his trembling knees. "Shift into Park, okay?"

"Right." He shut off the car completely.

"This has to be the last place you really want to be," Eve protested, measuring his granite profile with concern.

"It's necessary." He emerged from the car, taking in the area from behind the security of his tinted lenses. The bend in the roadside was no different than all the others up and down the mountainside. A stand of pines growing into the sky, brush and wildflowers at his feet. The drop-off point was easy to spot through the trees at this time of day, and a length of new guardrail reflected points of sunshine, marking the spot of their crash. Beyond it lay a steep, rocky ravine leading to the river's edge.

With cautious steps he moved forward.

"Careful!" Eve cried.

He lifted a hand in acknowledgment, as he picked his way through the trees. He forced himself to the rail, to stare down the steep incline. His senses opened wide to his surroundings: the rush of the water, a pair of cawing hawks overhead, the stiff breeze ruffling his hair, stinging his face. He would try to remember this daylight setting rather than the dark and ugly one.

"What are you doing?" Eve asked gently, tipping her head against his shoulder.

"Trying to remember. Trying to forget. Oh, I don't know, Eve! I feel like such a failure!"

"None of this is your fault, Jared."

"But I hit the brakes over and over again!" he lamented, pressing his fists into his eyes. "Nothing happened. Noth—" He broke off, his jaw dropping. "What did you call me?"

Eve huffed, clearly exasperated. "Please cut the act. I don't know the hows or whys, but I do know there was some kind switch at the plant upstairs. You are Jared Reed. *Finis.* For sure."

He eyed her with the respect she deserved. "Care to tell me where I went wrong?"

"All sorts of times," she said on a bubbly laughter. "Right from the start, when I fixed your coffee all wrong."

"You suspected even then?"

"Let's just say I filed all your mistakes away for future reference."

He exhaled heavily. "Guess you're too good for me."

"Tell me something I don't know! I mean the straight scoop now. What happened?"

With a rocking motion, he moved away from the rail. "As usual, I got into a mess pinch hitting for Sam. He was supposed to die at the wheel. I wasn't even supposed to be along."

"Why did you make the trip?"

"Because he seemed woozy, drunk if you like. Nobody else seemed to notice. He wasn't loud, or openly tossing 'em back. Guess years of friendship helped me read the signs."

"He might have had a few drinks before the dinner," Eve suggested. "He did sometimes when he was nervous."

"Yeah, that's true." He paused as his intuition nudged him. "I feel as if I know something important, as if something somebody said is trapped in the back of my head. But what?"

"It'll come to you. Stick to the story, please."

"There isn't much more to tell. I made a heavenly bargain to return in Sam's body to rejoin my family, only to find out my loving wife was ready to unload me."

Her face crumpled in sympathy. "How awful for you! I so wish you had confided in me right off the bat. I could've helped you through every step, made things a whole lot easier."

"I wanted Kate to be the first to know," he explained. "Unfortunately, she's been slow to decide whether our marriage was worth saving. So I've just been biding my time, carrying my secret."

"She sure knows you're different, though," Eve objected. "She has new and special feelings for you, too."

"That's true. But I would like the assurance that she'll be pleased with the news."

"You've stalled long enough, Jared. She's as ready as she'll ever be."

"I almost confessed Friday night. But we were out in the yard, it was late, and she was wearing only a coat."

Eve swiftly read between the lines, and was horrified. "You shouldn't have gone that far without telling her!"

"Didn't mean to. Didn't expect intimacy. But it was a mutual thing, Eve. If possible, Kate needed it more than I did."

Eve's thin arms flew in the air. "Ha! None of that matters. The deed is done! It's time you march right back into that car, fire it up and hightail it back to the city to make a full confession. This very instant, with the hope you haven't waited just a little too long!"

Eve entertained him all the way home with all the mistakes he'd made in his new identity. Not only did he drink his coffee wrong that first day, but she reminded him that he'd automatically gone to his old desk, and wanted her to open his cherished personal mail. To top it all off, he wasn't convincingly bonkers over Gretchen.

Jared soured over the mention of the crass blonde, but had to agree such behavior would've been expected of Sam. And then there was his seeking out of Kate, and the masterful way he handled her. Sam had always been a little afraid of the schoolteacher because she was so capable and bright. All in all, the pieces hadn't fit for Eve. Searching for some explanation, she'd found herself drawn to the subject of reincarnation.

Jared was mighty relieved to roll up in front of the redhead's town house. "Any last coal you'd like to drag me over?" he asked in good humor.

"Well, there was the issue of sex between us."

"You and Sam and sex!"

Eve laughed at his shell-shocked expression. "No, and that's my point. Sam and I never did the wild thing, you dopey bozo. Remember on Kate's step when I suggested we had and you didn't argue?"

"Oh, yeah."

"Of course what finally clinched my theory for good was the psychic transmission I sent you the other night, the one that brought you running to the office." She chuckled smugly. "I didn't call for Sam, I called for you,

Jared. Despite all I knew, I nearly lost it when you barreled through the door on command."

"Well, remind me never to lie to you again."

She blew him a parting kiss from the boulevard. "I think you're spooked enough to remember. Now get over to Kate's and beg for mercy."

Jared drove on with new confidence. Having someone to confide in, someone to prod him along was just the boost he needed.

"FOUND THE TARNISH remover," Kate announced, stepping onto her back deck with a bottle, a bowl and rag. She was still dressed in the mint green blouse and skirt she had worn on the flea market expedition. "It isn't the gooey stuff, either. You just dip your silver and presto, it's clean!"

Kate set her things on the table and sank into a brightly cushioned chair. "Where are Bonny and Martha?"

Walter gestured to the back of the yard, where Bonny was leading Martha, who was carrying an old straw tote bag, back toward the playhouse. "I engineered this time alone."

"Oh?" She smiled at him fondly as she poured some of the cleaner into the bowl.

"I want to speak to you about Sam."

"Oh." Her tone was flat, reflecting her disappointment. Her friendship with Sam was her business. Period.

"Bonny said he's here all the blasted time."

Kate dipped an old silver frame into the bowl, and chose her words with the same patience and care she was applying to her task. "I imagine my darling daughter has also told you what a valuable helper he's been."

He snorted.

Kate pursed her lips, struggling to control her temper. "I know you mean well, but . . . I think your road trip is just the diversion you need," she said diplomatically. "A chance to expand your interests."

To his credit, Walter had the grace to appear slightly contrite. "Katey, dear, don't shut me down as a nosy fuddy-duddy."

"But you're pushing too hard, Walt," she said gently but firmly. "Jared would want Sam here in our lives. There has to be plenty of good in him or Jared wouldn't have stood by him all these years."

"Well, maybe Jared was played for a fool all those years!"

Surging with annoyance, Kate tossed aside the frame with a clatter. "That's an awful thing to say!"

Walter settled in beside her at the slatted table, pushing the bowl of cleaner out of the way. "Hear me out. That's all I ask. I have new information that just might shed some light on a lot of things."

She regarded him anxiously. "One of your sources come through?"

His frown deepened. "Martha still plays golf in the league for the Metro force wives, you know."

Kate expressed surprise. "She got the scoop?"

"Don't know how she'll leave that circle of cacklers when we take off in that rattletrap trailer," he grumbled. "Anyway, they had their end-of-season luncheon yesterday, at the same lodge where they had my retirement party."

Which had nothing to do with anything, Kate was sure. But Walter could ramble, especially when he was upset.

"Anyway, the investigation came up courtesy of Louise Edgerton. She called at the crack of dawn to make sure Martha had some kind of booby prizes ready." Kate was sure they were door prizes, but let it slide. "In a stroke of luck the blabbermouth assumed that Martha still had access to all of Metro's moves. 'Course we know that's not so since my retirement, but Louise apparently doesn't. She's so accustomed to discussing shop with my wife, she brought up the search warrants Dennis had gotten from Judge Morehead the night before."

"And you in turn warned me."

He shook his balding head. "I never did that, young lady."

"Oh, yes," she said sheepishly. "Forgot myself."

"Louise is just the opposite of tightlipped Dennis," he rambled on. "No wonder they complement each other."

"Here comes Martha," Kate said with a measure of relief as the older woman glided across the grass in her bold floral blouse and matching skort. Finally, Kate would get some concise answers.

Martha waved a fleshy arm as she climbed the two shallow steps to the deck.

"Everything sound back there?" Walter asked pointedly.

Martha met his pale eyes with a twinkle. "Dandy. Bonny's sweeping her floor with the little broom we bought her." She sank into a nearby chair, with her clumsy bag in her lap. "Have you explained things to Kate yet? To her satisfaction, I mean?"

"Tryin', Ma."

Martha looked meaningfully in Kate's direction. "Figured I might be needed to fill in the blanks. Some people babble on and never get to the point."

The gibe went right over Walter's head. "Well, I told her all about Louise's blabbing," he assured her. "Got that far."

"So Louise spilled the news about the warrant," Kate prompted.

Martha nodded. "Yes, she told me that much on the phone. Didn't get any real answers until the luncheon a few hours later. Walter armed me with loads of questions to ask."

"And you did a wonderful job, dear," he congratulated heartily.

"One thing I don't understand is why they waited all these weeks to search this house," Kate said, annoyed and bewildered. "Lots can be shuffled around with every passing day."

Martha cleared her throat. "Louise said everything happening now was triggered by Sam's waking up, the answers he gave Dennis during questioning."

"Incomplete, evasive answers," Walter clarified. "To give Dennis his due, he was sure that Sam would clear things up. He was disappointed when he put Sam to the test and he flunked."

Kate remembered that Sam had said as much himself, but hearing it was really true, made it all the more nerve-racking. Her throat constricted as she tried to speak, making her speech scratchy. "What's the official version?"

"They hoped Sam would admit to having several pieces from the Carson Collection in his possession, and explain why. As we all know, he stuck to a story about having only the ruby ring. Apparently a diamond broach, an emerald bracelet, and some kind of pendant were found stashed under the Camaro's seat. Not that the stuff was worth a king's ransom, not by any means. It's valued at about two hundred grand, like the reward itself."

"Which brings us to their theories," Martha put in. "They believe Sam may have found the thief who took the collection in the first place. For reasons still unknown, he struck a blackmail deal with this person, settling for a share of the jewelry rather than the reward. Unfortunately, the possibility that Jared might have gone along with the plan is why your house was searched."

Kate pressed a hand to her chest with a small cry of indignation. "Jared? My Jared?"

"Dennis will clear him," Walter stated confidently. "He has to go through the motions because Jared was along for the ride and the ruby ring was found on his body."

Dread crowded Kate's chest, making breathing difficult. "So Sam is the central target of the probe?"

Walter patted Kate's hand. "Yes. His story just didn't wash."

"It made sense to me," Kate argued. "The guys went into the mountains to recover the entire collection! Sam even had twenty thousand dollars on him, that he intended to use as a payoff!"

"The cash could've been merely a cover to back up Sam's claim, in case Jared or someone else stumbled upon his blackmail scheme. Don't forget, he was surrounded by officers all night long at my party. He was accustomed to measuring all the angles. Looking for the quickest shortcut."

"Blackmail's a shortcut?" she cried in challenge.

Walter's arched brow betrayed his annoyance over her attitude, but he kept his voice even. "Sometimes. Presumably Sam solved this case, and then came to realize that bringing the guilty party to justice would be a lot of hassle. Could be somebody prominent or somebody attractive who appealed to his greed and vanity. Who knows?"

Kate's mouth gaped. "So who sliced the brakeline?"

"The blackmail victim of course. He handed over a fraction of the jewels and then planned the murder to end the blackmail for good."

Kate kept her chin high and steady. "I believe Sam's version."

"Oh, Katey, are you willing to bet your life on it? Bonny's life, too?"

Walter did have a way of cutting through the sentiment. Kate stood on shaky legs, hurt and mystified.

Walter shot up to block her path. "This isn't the reaction I expected of you, Kate. Where's your moral outrage? There's a real possibility here that Sam Stone destroyed your happiness through his own selfish greed!"

Kate knew she couldn't begin to match Walt's fury. Not yet. Of course that fact only made him all the angrier. "Don't you have even a smidgen of faith in Sam, Walt?"

"Faith? In that two-bit hustler?" Walter's large face quivered. "He wasn't worthy to shine Jared's shoes. I'm not a bit surprised by this tragic ending. I—" Walter choked, as though his tongue had expanded. "I only put up with him because of you and Jared."

Kate was no longer sure what was holding her up. Her whole body was jelly. "You always seemed to like Sam," she protested. "Every bit as much as Jared."

"I wanted you kids to be happy, Katey, wanted Valley View Investigations to support you well. That's why I tolerated that smart-ass ladykiller the best I could, acted as his station house source, too."

"How extraordinary," she murmured.

Walter cleared his throat, and gave her a short, fierce hug. "I figured we shared that opinion of Sam."

"I struggle with my opinions on people," she said, choosing her words with care, thinking of her seesawing feelings for Jared that the Helsers knew nothing about. "I try to readjust my views when necessary, give second chances when deserved. Have faith."

Walter's eyes glittered with certainty. "Old man like me doesn't bother. To me Sam's always been just a punk hustler, who's grown into a common killer who's run out of chances. You think about it."

Kate needed relief from his penetrating eyes, so she looked away, toward the patio screen door. To her horror she saw movement in the house. There was Sam, eavesdropping on every word!

Despite these new very logical assertions of Walter's, she wanted nothing more than to comfort the man who had comforted her, without expectations, without strings, without questions.

She smoothed her clothing. "I need a minute alone," she announced tersely. "Please. Stay out here with Bonny. I'll be right back."

It took all her self-control to ease through the sliding-glass door with any dignity. She broke into a run as soon as she'd cleared the kitchen, and caught him in the driveway. He tried to edge behind the wheel of the car, but she blocked his way.

"I'm so sorry you had to hear that," she cried breathlessly.

He braced his hand on the roof of the car just over her shoulder, and spoke through gritted teeth. "So am I."

"You should've stormed out there, made a fuss, set him straight!"

How could he, when he still didn't know what had gone on himself? "I don't have enough ammo to fight him yet," he told her honestly.

"Wouldn't it have helped to just have your say?" She grasped his sinewy arms and gave him an ineffectual shake.

"Bullying an old retired cop is a useless exercise I don't need," he said succinctly. "I'm busy with the real police." He couldn't tell her how shell-shocked he was. How speechless he was. Poor Sam had always liked the Helsers.

"Did you learn anything at the tavern?" she asked on a softer note.

He exhaled to calm himself. "Not much. Like Dennis told me, a dark truck was spotted next to the Camaro at one point. And Wayne, the owner, said he'd seen a man and woman get into the truck on another occasion."

"Things add up to a partnership," she concluded. "We're getting there."

"Kate, the cops think I'm a dirty blackmailer!"

"Yes." She released her grip on him, and wove her fingers together nervously.

He studied her intently, drilling his eyes into her deep purple ones. Knowing himself how easy lies could come when needed, he didn't give a rip what she had to say. He wanted the story behind the story; her gut reaction to the whole thing. It didn't take long for it to surface. She was afraid and doubtful. And all in all, he couldn't blame her.

Without another word, he left.

12

"YOUR LIFE IS going down the tubes and you're repairing this old maple desk." Eve flung her arms wide in despair.

"Working with my hands relaxes me," Jared replied tightly.

"All you said on the phone was that everything was kaput. Are you Jared Reed or Bob Vila?"

"Here, hold these joints together while I glue them."

"So, you tell Kate? She throw you out?"

That got through Jared's shell of indifference. He sank back on the floor, raising his knees, burying his face in his arms.

She sank down beside him. "If you don't tell me the story, I can't help you."

So he did. Every rotten word Walter had said.

Eve blinked in wonder. "I had no idea that Walter hated Sam."

"Neither did I. It would've hurt him terribly."

"I take it you left without telling Kate the truth?"

He glared at her. "Use your head. Kate was already a mess. He'd shaken her trust in me. What if she decided I was trying to duck out of trouble by claiming I was Jared? And don't you think Walter would've come charging in to shut me down?"

"Guess you do have some points." She sat cross-legged in front of him and fell silent for a spell. "Say, you don't think that Sam may have . . . I mean, can we be sure he didn't?"

"He was innocent, Eve! I am willing to risk everything on that assumption. He was just a big kid at heart. He even doted on Mrs. Ginty across the hall."

"Okay, just trying to be thorough. So, what do we do now?"

"I've been thinking about that," he said, a glimmer of new life in his green eyes. "I say if we can't beat 'em, we have to try and join 'em. C'mon, we're going for a ride."

"NICE CROP, DENNIS."

"Sam. Eve." The chunky detective froze in the center of his backyard vegetable garden, clenching the handle of his hoe. "What a surprise."

Jared and Eve exchanged a wry look. They were as welcome as a blast of hellfire.

Using his hoe as a walking stick Dennis gingerly made his way between the neat rows of vegetables. He stepped clumsily over the knee-high wire fencing. "Forgot you know where I live."

"Don't have to sound so grumpy about it," Eve said sassily, bracing a hand on her hip.

"We need to talk," Jared began. "And I'm sure I'll be stepping on toes."

Dennis's small eyes glimmered. "You wish to make a statement?"

"No, I don't wish to make a statement," Jared mimicked.

"Then why are you bugging me on a Sunday? Louise is at some committee shindig, the kids are off playing albums. This is my quality time."

"CDs," Eve corrected triumphantly. "The kids don't play albums anymore, they play CDs."

Dennis ripped off his fabric work gloves with a sputter. "What in hell do you idiots want?"

"To show you you don't know everything!" Eve retorted. "Albums. Jeez."

"We want to save an innocent man's life!" Jared exclaimed, stepping in front of Eve.

Dennis's brows arched, then fell. "Oh. You mean yours, don't you?"

"As it happens, yes."

He lead them to a cement slab patio behind the white Colonial-style house, and gestured to some cast-iron lawn furniture. "Have a seat. Have your say."

Jared arranged his chair so that the three of them were in a semicircle. "I wouldn't spill this if my ass weren't on the line."

Dennis slapped his gloves against his knee. "I got that much straight on my own."

Jared gave him a tight smile. "Louise spilled her guts to Martha Helser."

"Say what!"

"About your case against me."

"That blabby old fool." Dennis muttered some choice comments about his wife. "How'd you find out what Louise said?"

"By accident," Jared explained. "Walter was telling Kate to look out for me and figured he needed to bring out the cannons to convince her. I happened to overhear."

Dennis flushed in anger and embarrassment.

"He's no blackmailer," Eve scolded. "Of all the dumb stunts for a promotion!"

Jared patted her knee in warning. "I'm going to level with you, Dennis," he said evenly. "I got the whole pitch, about the extra jewelry in the car and everything. I really think it was planted by whoever cut the brakeline. That person most likely took away the map then, too, to make it look like the meet was Sam's idea in the first place."

Dennis measured them, his lower lip drooping. "I've constructed my theory with care, weighed it against the evidence. Contrary to what you might think, I'd never railroad you or anybody else to get a promotion."

"Eve's snappy cause she's scared for me," Jared apologized. "But don't you see that if we do this right, you'll end up with the job and crook? On the other hand," he cautioned, "you drill me into the ground and you're going to lose. I'm the wrong man."

"Hope you are."

Jared's face lit up with a knowing smile. "Admit it, you've reached a dead end. Haven't you?"

Dennis worked his jaw. "Maybe."

"Well, together we can jumpstart this case again, I guarantee it."

"You got a plan?" Dennis asked doubtfully.

"I have a trap all set to go."

"What's it going to cost me?"

"All I really want, Dennis, is a ring."

Dennis winced in pain. "Oh, crap, you sound just like my wife does every anniversary. And it's never all she really wants."

"I APPRECIATE YOU folks coming over on Labor Day." Jared opened his front door wide the following afternoon to admit Ida and Mickey.

Ida waltzed into the room with authoritative briskness. "You were wise to call me. Rearranging furniture is right up my alley. I certainly deal with enough of it on the job. Have acquired a real knack for what works in a room. I—"

A rap on the door interrupted Ida's flow. She marched up to answer it. "Why, it's you!" she cried indignantly. "Lose some more of your underwear?"

"Now, Ida," Jared cautioned. "Gretchen is my guest, too."

Gretchen sashayed inside, dressed in a clingy orange dress more suitable for buying furniture than moving it. Jared was kind of surprised when she didn't cuddle up. But then he noticed the sparks between her and Ida's "boy wonder." No question that Gretchen was playing up to the kid.

Ida was intent on taking another run at Gretchen when Dennis Edgerton's stout figure loomed in the hallway. The sight of a stranger defused the housekeeper.

"This is my friend, Dennis. Insisted on helping with the heavier stuff."

The police detective nodded, scanning the group with a practiced eye. Jared had given him a complete rundown on each one, and had offered motives to consider.

Eve opened the door moments later. "Hope I'm not late," she chirped, scooting up to cuddle Dennis. "When Sam told me you were coming, Denny, I was thrilled. It's been too long."

Dennis smiled grimly, and put his mouth next to her ear. "How does a ten to twenty stretch in the pen sound for being a damned nuisance to society?"

"Now, Denny," Eve cooed loud enough for all to hear. "We need your brawn, not your great wit."

Ida patted her salt-and-pepper nest of hair, surveying Eve with motherly concern. "Incense rots the brain, I've tried to tell you."

"So, Sam," Dennis prodded, "what do you have in mind?"

Jared could see that the policeman was anxious to put their trap in motion. Jared had gathered them together on the pretext of rearranging the apartment, hoping to flush out their crook using the ruby ring as bait. The public had no idea that the ring—much less the Carson Collection—had any link to the car crash. Only the person who'd tried to set Sam up would know the ring's value and its meaning, and hopefully conclude that the cops had failed to make the link between Sam and the museum pieces. Jared reasoned that the culprit was persistent and would take the ring back for a second attempt to place blame on Sam.

Even Dennis had to admit the trap had potential, if Sam wasn't a dirty liar.

They spent the next hour pushing things around the living room and bedroom, looking for just the right effect. Somehow, Sam seemed impossible to satisfy.

He inhaled sharply when Gretchen cornered him at the kitchen sink. "Here you are."

"Just having a glass of water." He toasted her and took a sip.

"I hoped to catch you alone," she said a bit nervously.

"Oh?" He set the glass on the counter, and grasped her soft upper arms because it was the subtlest way to keep her hands off him.

"I think it's time for some honesty."

Jared swallowed in surprise. "Fire away."

Gretchen's ample bust rose and fell under her tight knit dress. "I'm not sure I love you anymore, steel tushie."

"No?"

"Why you even changed the locks on me."

She looked so forlorn he couldn't help smiling gently. "Not on you personally, Gretchen."

"You mean, there's lots of other girls?"

"Lots of other keys," he corrected gently. "I couldn't afford to have people walking in and out of my place anymore, not when I believe somebody's trying to hurt me."

She nodded her bright blond head. "That makes me feel better, but still I think we should break up. I've got another man who likes me a teensy bit more than you."

Mickey. Ida would have her hands full.

"Anyway, I just thought I'd get all my stuff together now."

He nodded, with a regretful sigh. "Whatever's best."

"I wouldn't want you to feel all broken up later just 'cause one of my bras popped into your face by surprise."

He controlled his twitching mouth with effort. "See what you mean. And thanks for being up front."

Dennis barged into the kitchen as Gretchen was leaving. It seemed to Jared that the detective took an immoderate amount of time edging past her. "Okay, hotshot, I've had enough. You tell this crowd the chairs all jive. I'm outta here in ten minutes."

"The ring still in my dresser?" Jared whispered.

"I don't know. Mickey's been lying on your bed for twenty minutes. The kid's not worth a whit, is he?"

Jared complied with Dennis's orders, being as casual as possible. Before long he had Ida, Mickey and Gretchen filing out the door. Poor Ida had positioned her body between the two. Jared mused that she'd be about as effective as a toothpick in a closing vise.

The moment the door closed, Eve raced to the bedroom. "It's gone, all right!"

Dennis charged to the cupboard where he'd hidden his walkie-talkie. He hit the on switch, and the box crackled to life as he moved to the window facing the street. An unmarked squad car sat at the curb. "It's me. Operation Ruby is a green light. Move in on all three."

"Operation Ruby?" Jared repeated with a chuckle.

"It works," Dennis barked with frayed patience. But he was very pleased and excited. Jared could tell.

Eve swayed up to him with a smirk. "Shoulda been Ruby Red to Emerald Green, Denny."

Dennis bobbed his head with a dangerous chuckle. "If I wasn't such a sweet guy, I'd drag you downtown for being a pain." He turned to Jared. "So, you coming downtown for the questioning? I'll let you eavesdrop on the box through the two-way mirror."

"No, I'm going over to Kate's. I want to tell her about this."

"What, that you broke up with Barbie doll!" Dennis slapped him on the back with a hearty laugh.

"Among other things," Jared admitted, filled with relief and pleasure.

"Well, just so I know where to reach you."

"I will want a report as soon as you have something concrete," Jared thought to add.

Dennis poked him in the chest. "Just don't expect any of the credit." The walkie-talkie he'd set on the table began to crackle. He picked it up and moved back over to the window. "What is it, Mike?"

"Gave the trio a weapons search down here and found the ring in the blonde's purse. Should I let the other two go?"

"They're as interwoven as hillbilly cousins. Run 'em all down to the precinct," Dennis ordered. "I'll be right after you."

13

"KATE, HE'S HERE again!" Walter bellowed, stomping into the Reed kitchen an hour later. "Don't that boy have a home of his own?"

Kate was at the kitchen broom closet, plucking a chef's apron off a hook inside. She put the front loop over her head and smoothed the white cover-up over her tan slacks and blue top. "Tie my strings, will you?" Walter shuffled up and secured the apron at her waist with fumbling fingers.

"What's all the commotion about?" Martha eased inside the patio door, wearing a printed dress that matched her husband's shirt.

"Sam would show up on our last day in town!"

Martha remained chipper. "Oh, Walt, so what?"

"Show you what." Walter stormed down the hallway, the women in his wake.

"Sam has always been welcome at our Labor Day barbecue," Kate called after him.

Walter barged out onto the stoop just as Jared approached the silver-domed trailer parked in the driveway. "What are you doin'?" he roared.

Jared froze in his tracks. "Just wanted to have a look inside," he called back pleasantly.

Kate appeared on the stoop. "Come in, Sam. You can light the barbecue for me."

Balling his fists, Walter turned on his heel and charged back inside the house.

Kate shifted uncomfortably as Sam joined her on the stoop. "Sorry about that."

He could tell she meant it. Despite Walter's accusations, she still hung on to her faith in him. "To be honest, I wanted you all to myself, too."

"They'll be gone in a couple of hours," she consoled. "Just came to say goodbye before the big journey. After that, I'm all yours. Okay?"

His eyes crinkled affectionately. "Best offer I've had since Friday night."

She flushed. "When you didn't call today, I felt lost."

He enveloped her slender hands in his huge ones. "I was busy with the case. Dennis and I joined forces to set a trap at the apartment."

"Oh?" There was lilt in her voice, suggesting she would welcome something that would clear him. He hated that she needed it, but until she knew he was Jared, it was only natural.

"The cops caught Gretchen red-handed with the ruby," he reported. "She had the nerve to carry it out in her purse."

She clapped her hands together. "Oh, Sam, that's wonderful! I can't wait to tell Walter. Throw some crow on the barbecue for him."

"Let me tell him, Kate. I want to make the most of it."

By the time Jared and Kate reached the kitchen the Helsers were out on the deck with Bonny.

Jared wandered over to the kitchen table where Kate had set out the ribs and a bowl of her special sauce. He picked up the basting brush, dipped it in the bowl and began to coat the meat. If he didn't keep his hands busy, he'd go crazy. "Walter know I overheard his tirade yesterday?"

Kate was standing at the cupboard, near the sink, counting out dinner plates. "No. It just seemed better to let him set sail on his trip."

Jared stared out the window facing the deck. Walter was busy lighting the grill himself. The old coot was impossible. When Kate finally took the platter of meat outside, Walter insisted on doing the barbecuing and demanded Kate's apron. She gave it up in good humor. Jared was beginning to think she'd missed her calling. Surely the United Nations could use such a patient diplomat, especially one who could cry on cue to get information.

The telephone rang then. Jared strolled over to the wall to pick it up.

It was for Sam.

He tipped his shoulder against the door frame, listening to Dennis Edgerton's hostile flood. "Gretchen says I told her she could have the ring?" Jared cut in. "No, I told her she could collect her personal stuff, the perfume and panties. You overheard our talk."

"She says you promised it to her the day before the accident."

"Before?" he whispered, keeping his eye on the patio door.

"The day you claim it arrived at Mrs. Ginty's, remember?"

"Wow, what an operator!"

"If this is some kind of trick, I'll slap the cuffs on you right now!"

"How'd she explain lifting my answering machine tape, and sifting through my mail?"

"She says they were the acts of a jealous lover."

"But it all clicks too well, Dennis—Gretchen luring Mickey into the scheme. He has the mechanical background, and a young man played messenger to Mrs. Ginty."

"I know it! But Gretchen's a convincing bimbo. If she's guilty, she belongs in the cinema."

"They don't say cinema anymore. They say movies." A crease marred his forehead as he thought. "You aren't springing her, are you?"

Dennis growled over the line. "Not yet. But, Sam, she said I should ask you, so I'm asking, did you ever say she could have that ring?"

Jared paused. Sam wouldn't have said something that stupid. "That very ring?" he questioned. "Go back and ask her exactly what I said."

"Why not tell me yourself!"

"Because I'm having a little trouble with my memory since the coma, that's why!" With a gruff sound, he hung up. Kate was tensely pacing the deck, so he wandered outside with a couple of glasses of soda to see if he could rescue her from Walter.

"Walter, you're going to burn those ribs to dust," he teased.

Walter turned, homing in on the glasses in his hands. "You're wrong, boy. One of your drunken hazes, I bet."

As Jared handed Kate one of the sodas a light clicked on in a far corner of his mind, shining on things from a different angle—the conversation with Mrs. Ginty, the evening at Shooter's.... He excused himself, needing some time alone to think.

They ate shortly thereafter. The ribs were beef jerky tough, and the salad dressing a little soupy. Apparently Martha, nervous over her husband's bad temper, had added a little too much buttermilk to her prize dressing recipe. Bonny, too young to understand table tact, gave up on the meal, grabbed a handful of potato chips, and dashed back to her playhouse.

The telephone rang in the midst of dessert. The apple pie was delicious, made by Kate ahead of time, hours before the friction started.

"I'll get that." Jared rose from his chair.

Unfortunately, Kate was closer to the sliding door. "I'll do it." Dabbing her mouth with her napkin, she dashed off with Bonny's kind of energy.

Certain it was Dennis, Jared remained standing.

Kate returned to confirm the fact. "No, don't bother to rush. He's gone now."

"What did he say?"

"He's planning to stop by later. And, boy, did he sound mad."

"That tears it!" Walter bulleted to his feet, throwing down his napkin. "We're leaving."

"But, Walter!" Martha clicked her tongue, gesturing to her large straw tote bag. "I promised Bonny I'd visit her little house one last time, as a door-to-door cosmetics saleswoman."

Walter's enraged features smoothed. "Okay, Marthy."

"And we'll clear the table for Kate, won't we?" she added, waiting for Walter's affirmation. "After all, dear, if they're coming to arrest Sam, that is none of our affair, is it?"

"Martha!" Jared thundered at the prim old woman.

The retired teacher smiled faintly. "I personally don't believe you've done a blessed thing wrong. But I have to think about Walter's blood pressure. You and Kate can understand that. He has to slow down, get away from stress."

Sounded like a good remedy for all of them. Jared stepped away from the table, and walked down the steps into the yard. Poor Kate, he thought. She looked about ready to crumple. Her friendly little family circle was a blazing ring of fire.

The Helsers did indeed clear the table. As the clatter of plates and running water wafted through the window above the sink, Jared resisted the urge to go in for kitchen duty. Instead he strolled around the lawn, picking up tree branches, listening in on Bonny's chatter. Things seemed to be clinking in her playhouse, too, and he wondered if she, too, was pretending to clean up. The sun was just setting, leaving the sky streaked with pinks and yellows.

Dennis probably expected to find him shivering in his shoes, but Jared welcomed his arrival. He had all the pieces in place now.

Dusk was settling in when Jared saw movement near the service door of the garage. The motion-sensitive yard light flicked on, efficiently illuminating the entire backyard. To Jared's disappointment, it was only Walter. He marched forward with purpose.

"You been poking 'round in my mobile home?"

"No offense, Walter. Just took a quick tour."

"You know, you really got a nerve, hanging around here when the cops are coming for you. Think you'd have more respect for Kate and Bonny. Why, if Jared were here—"

"What would Jared do?" Jared had reached the end of his rope and it showed. His green eyes glittered dangerously. They stood in a enraged standoff for a long, sizzling moment.

"Look at me!" Bonny squeaked excitedly, racing out of her playhouse. "I'm going to a fancy party!"

The men turned slowly in unison toward the child skipping in their direction.

She was dripping in jewelry. Gaudy gold jewelry. Bonny had somehow uncovered the missing pieces of the Carson Collection.

"Damn and blast," Walter muttered. He raised a halting palm toward the child. "Don't move, Bonny, dear." The child froze in obedience. "Martha!" he barked toward the kitchen window.

It was Kate who clattered out onto the deck. A small scream of surprise escaped her mouth before she clamped her hand over it.

"What's the matter with everybody?" Bonny asked in a frightened peep.

Kate quickly crossed the lawn to join Bonny, and curved an arm across her shoulders. "Where did you get this jewelry?"

"In my playhouse. It was hidden in the wall. A hunk of wood fell down and I saw a bag." She shook her finger at Jared. "You gotta nail things better, Uncle Sammy."

Kate's gaze met Jared's for a long, panicky moment.

"You dirty scoundrel," Walter growled, backing toward Bonny and Kate, his arms spread like a protective bear. "No wonder he wanted to fix up that playhouse, Kate. No wonder."

"Don't listen to him, Kate," Jared pleaded. "He's twisting this to make me look bad."

Martha emerged from the garage with her straw tote bag. "What's this nonsense?"

"See for yourself, Marthy," Walter said furiously. "Sam Stone eliminates Jared, then moves in to use his girls."

Bonny huddled close to Kate. "What's liminate, Mommy?"

"Well . . ." Kate began bleakly.

"It means Sam killed your daddy!" Walter blustered.

"Daddy!" The child promptly burst into tears.

Walter crooked his finger at her. "You come to Walter, dear. I need a huggy."

"Kate!" Jared shouted. "Don't let her go!"

Openly confused, Kate kept a firm grip on Bonny's shoulders.

"It's no use, Walter," Jared said firmly, taking a step closer. "I've figured out everything."

"Figured you're headed for jail!" Walter shook his head forcefully. "Kate sees through you now. She was temporarily smitten, but that's all."

"What happened that night at the museum, Walter? You plan the robbery with the guard in advance? He have an unexpected heart attack? How convenient that you were first on the scene. At Valley View, we always thought that was interesting. Funny, eh? We were trying to track down that collection with you and your departmental resources and you had the jewelry all the time. I could die laughing."

"You just might." Walter reached into Martha's straw bag and produced his service revolver. "Keep your distance, Kate. This guy is as deadly as they come."

"And what are the chances that Martha intended to load the jewelry into that bag of hers tonight when Kate put Bonny to bed? Play the cosmetic sales game, then push her out the door to brush her teeth? That's why you're still here, because Martha couldn't manage to get into that playhouse without Bonny. How nervous you two must have been when I arrived. And then on top of it, Dennis has decided to join the party."

"You have a load of nothin', Stone!" Walter shouted fiercely.

"You really had me fooled for a while," Jared went on. "Didn't think you could hurt any of us, so I never considered you. But then the tables started to turn. I found out you hated Sam. So I got to piecing other things together. Mrs. Ginty said the messenger was young. But everybody's young to her. She called me 'boy.' You called me 'boy' today. Older people do that.

"Then there was our pool game at Shooter's. You mentioned Sam was in a drunken haze at your party. So upset, so trusting, it passed me by for days. But nobody could've known that, unless he'd drugged Sam's drink. Oh, and this folksy tour of the country. What a great way to cross the Canadian border. Ditch the trailer up there and hop a flight to . . . well, not the Bahamas, cause when Sam didn't die, you had to frame him with those tickets Martha bought, didn't you? But there are lots of other warm places to retire in, where those gems can be sold for their real worth. My guess is, you already have a buyer in mind, Walter. You've always been so thorough."

"Don't you believe a word of this, Kate," Martha chortled in her classroom voice. "Why the man's insane, referring to himself in the third person. Who does he think he is? Sherlock Holmes? Now you and Bonny come closer, so Walter can shield you with his weapon."

Jared's heart slammed hard against his chest. This was it. The moment of truth. He couldn't let Walter get his hands on Bonny. She'd make an ideal hostage, and he could snap the child's neck with a quick crack. He raised his hands as Kate cuddled Bonny close in her trembling arms. "Listen carefully, Kate. This wasn't the way I intended to break this news to you, but I'm not Sam at all. I'm Jared."

Walter's booming laugh filled the air. "This is the limit!"

"It's true. Think hard. Haven't I been acting more like your husband than the Sam you knew?"

She nodded, her eyes wide with astonishment.

"You ask Bonny, didn't I know where my sunglasses were in our bedroom, didn't I call her my Bonny bunny?"

"Did he, Bonny?" she asked hoarsely.

"Oh, Mommy!" The child sobbed against her chest. "I don't understand!"

And neither did Kate. Jared could see this was more than she was able to accept.

"If he is indeed Jared, why didn't he say so sooner?" Martha challenged.

"Because you wanted the divorce, Kate," Jared swiftly replied. "Remember in the park, when I thought you were pregnant? Remember how devastated I was over the truth? Oh, honey, I've just been biding my time, looking for a good opportunity to break the news."

"Kate," Martha intervened, "you aren't susceptible to this sort of foolishness."

"Eve figured it out," Jared told Kate. "Now, didn't she hint that something big was going on?"

"Yes," Kate admitted, wavering. "But what about the trap for Gretchen?"

"That's why Dennis called, because Gretchen had answers for everything. Naturally, I didn't know all of Sam's moves before his death, and apparently I was wrong about her. Now it seems likely that Gretchen saw the ring at the apartment, and Sam, counting on the reward money, promised her one like it. She must've taken it from the dresser today as some kind of consolation prize."

"Kate," Walter barked, "enough is enough. Let's take Bonny into the house."

"Oh, sure, and you'll get close enough to grab her. I can hear that trailer engine running." Jared's gaze sharpened lethally. "You stop and think, old man. Bonny isn't some kid I like, she's the daughter I love. It's Sam you despised, Sam who didn't measure up in your eyes. I'm as sharp as you've always believed. Understand who you're dealing with." Kate took two steps closer to the Helsers and he whirled on her, struggling to keep his voice level. "Listen carefully, honey. Remember at the travel agency. Let go and use your instincts."

"Oh, Sam—Jared. Whoever you are!" She squeezed Bonny harder, tears springing to her eyes. "I just don't want my baby hurt."

Jared inhaled deeply. "Kate, remember in the hallway?"

She shook her head, her mouth parting. "Oh, no, please don't . . ."

"Just remember," he urged. "Wasn't it just like the Fourth of July? Our first Fourth of July?"

"Oh, my... it is you. It has to be you!" In a frantic rush, Kate raced for him, dragging Bonny with her.

"Stop!" Walter cocked his gun and aimed it at Kate and Bonny. With screams and cries, they froze.

Finally confident that Kate trusted him, Jared wasted no more time. "Back way off, honey," he ordered, waving her away. "There's nothing he can do if he can't catch you."

"But, Jared—"

"He isn't going to shoot anybody. Just run from all of us. Call 9-1-1." To his relief, Kate steered Bonny in a wide circle toward the house.

Walter did pull the trigger then, as Jared advanced on him. But nothing happened. Jared wrenched the gun from his trembling hand and tossed it aside. "I emptied this thing an hour ago, Walter. Ain't a bullet left in the whole damn trailer."

Dennis Edgerton came around the corner of the garage just as Jared punched Walter in the jaw. He teetered back to the ground. Martha was instantly at his side, stroking his forehead. Jared stood over them, and his voice broke when he spoke. "That's for Sam, you bastard. He loved you, man. He really did."

Epilogue

"ARE WE SURE we want a green roof, Daddy?"

Jared gazed down from his perch atop the playhouse the following afternoon as he hammered in the last shingle. "We are sure, Bonny bunny. Very, very, sure."

Bonny turned to Eve, who was studying the effect with the frown of a temperamental artist. "Well, Evey?"

Jared's brow lifted like a raven's wing as he handed his hammer and nails down to the perky redhead.

"It's just perfect," Eve enthused, ruffling Bonny's blond head.

With a satisfied nod Jared eased off the roof.

"Hey, here comes Mom!" Bonny waved her hands high above her head as Kate strolled through the grass dressed in a simple gray suit, still clutching her briefcase.

"How was school?" Jared asked, kissing her temple.

She laughed wearily. "First days are always rough."

"I had a good first day," Bonny reported. "Picked out my desk."

Kate nodded. "And things are bound to get better as the week wears on."

"House is finished," Jared announced.

"Let's set up a tea party," Eve suggested. She steered Bonny inside, winking at Kate.

Jared enveloped his wife in a huge bear hug, groaning from the pit of his belly.

"It feels so good to be home," she murmured, splaying her hands across his soft white T-shirt.

"Does it ever," he heartily agreed, and captured her mouth for a deep kiss.

Kate sagged against his chest as she came up for air. "Did you speak to Dennis today?"

"Yeah, Walter broke down. Everything I figured was true. He was behind the robbery, in cahoots with the museum guard. As their getaway grew closer, he wanted to muddy the waters, get the cops going in another direction."

"So he set up the phony deal with Sam?"

"Yup. Once we got to the tavern, he sliced Sam's brakeline, took away the map, and planted the extra pieces of jewelry."

Kate's expression was full of misery. "But he knew you were along, Jared. He knew you'd die."

"Yes," he agreed sadly. "In the end, he was willing to sacrifice me, too. But if it's any consolation, I believe he and Martha have always cared for you—for our family. Greed just began to eat them whole. I imagine, like a lot of people, they'd worked hard all their lives and hadn't hit the jackpot. Walter saw retirement looming and came up with the plot to rob the museum. The guard had a weak heart and his part in the theft proved too much for him. Anyway, Martha was ready and waiting outside for the jewelry. Walter passed it to her, waited a short time, then triggered the alarm. He stayed, claiming to be first on the scene."

"They should've just left town in that damn mobile home!" Kate lamented.

"I know. They probably would've made a clean get-away with the whole collection. But Walter was obsessed with leaving a cold trail. He honestly believed Sam's life to be worthless, that nobody would miss him."

She grew solemn. "Poor Sam."

"Yeah. But as I told you, he's doing fine." He gazed up at the bright blue sky. "Somewhere out there."

"And we're doing fine." Kate snuggled closer. "Oh, darling, the more I think about the things I've said to you this past week, the more self-conscious I am. How hurt you must've been when I wouldn't admit to wanting you back."

He tapped the tip of her nose. "You think too much!"

"Yes, but that isn't all bad. After some soul-searching I can confidently say that had you told me the truth the night we made love, I would've been ready to hear it, thrilled to hear it."

"As rough as this journey home has been, I've got to say, I've never felt closer to you. Our friendship has deepened to new levels. It's wonderful."

She beamed in agreement. "So, have you decided who you're going to be, Jared or Sam?"

"I think from a legal standpoint, it would be easier to keep on as Sam. We can get married for appearances' sake, and take it from there."

"All right by me."

"If you don't mind, though, when we're in bed . . ."

"You want me to call you Jared?"

"Dreamboat."

"Oh, dear." She giggled madly. "I forgot about that!"

"It would mean a lot, really. All the time you were carrying on in that travel agency, I was wishing it was over me."

"Okay, any other crazy requests?"

"Well, we do have to decide how to spend our half of the reward money. The cool hundred grand."

"How's Eve spending hers?"

Jared shrugged nonchalantly. "Incense, a new car, things like that."

"Guess our needs are different," she conceded. "You have any ideas?"

He tugged her against his length and rubbed his body against hers suggestively. "Only one," he crooned in her ear.

"That's free."

Jared chuckled lovingly. "I'm talking about making a baby, baby."

"I know," she admitted coyly. "And it's your most heavenly idea yet."

This month's irresistible novels from

Temptation®

A MAN FROM OKLAHOMA by Lisa Harris

Rebels and Rogues

Undercover cop Jake Good Thunder and Julie FitzJames once shared an explosive relationship—but every day she'd feared for his life and she couldn't bear it. So she'd left him. Now, she needs his help and Jake has to decide if rekindling the flame is worth getting burned again...

THE HIGHWAYMAN by Madeline Harper

Rogues

Notorious highwayman Gabriel Stratton hungered for revenge, but it took Olivia Johnson, a mysterious woman from the future, to make him see that vengeance would only be the death of him. Olivia couldn't help falling for this rogue; her life would never be the same again...

COMMITMENTS by Susan Worth

Charlie Whitman did exactly as he pleased, all the time. He was committed to only one thing—no commitments! As Cassie Armstrong took *everything* seriously, they both thought that working together would be impossible! The fiery chemistry between them proved only one thing: opposites attract!

HEAVEN-SENT HUSBAND by Leandra Logan

Jared Reed had a lot to do—win back his wife, Kate, and discover who had tried to kill him and his partner, Sam. After the accident, Jared got a second chance—in the body of the handsome but sleazy Sam. Now he could have any woman he wanted. But he wanted Kate, and Kate had always disliked Sam...

Spoil yourself next month
with these four novels from

Temptation ®

STRANGER IN THE NIGHT by Roseanne Williams

The whole country thought Rafe Jermain died a traitor. But five years after their first encounter, Terra Camden finds out that he's very much alive and in need of her help. How can she refuse? He did save her life and he is the father of her son...

OBSESSION by Debra Carroll

Secret Fantasies

The last thing erotic-thriller writer Emma Jordan wants is any kind of relationship. But working with sexy-as-sin Sam Cooper creates a backdrop of sexual tension that makes the two of them burn with desire. Emma wants to keep her fantasies just that. *Fantasies*. But Sam is a hard man to resist...

LUCK OF THE DRAW by Candace Schuler

Mail Order Men

By the time Travis Holt discovered that his foreman had placed an ad to find him a wife, it was too late. Eve Reardon was on his doorstep, baby in arms, looking to marry him. Even if Travis hadn't needed her to care for his nieces, he wouldn't send her away—she did something to his insides... She made him *want* her...

WANTED! by JoAnn Ross

Men of Whiskey River

When Jessica Ingersoll rescues a wounded man who claims he's on a mission to avenge a murder over a hundred years old, she is unsurprisingly sceptical! But Rory Mannion was a rough and rugged lawman unlike any man she's ever met. If what he said was true, could they ever have a future together?

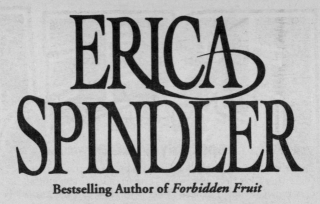

ERICA SPINDLER

Bestselling Author of *Forbidden Fruit*

FORTUNE

BE CAREFUL WHAT YOU WISH FOR... IT JUST MIGHT COME TRUE

Skye Dearborn's wishes seem to be coming true, but will Skye's new life prove to be all she's dreamed of—or a nightmare she can't escape?

"A high adventure of love's triumph over twisted obsession."

—*Publishers Weekly*

"Give yourself plenty of time, and enjoy!"

—*Romantic Times*

AVAILABLE IN PAPERBACK FROM JULY 1997

FREE!

FOUR FREE
specially selected
Temptation® novels
<u>PLUS</u> a FREE Mystery Gift
when you return this page...

Return this coupon and we'll send you 4 Temptation novels and a mystery gift absolutely FREE! We'll even pay the postage and packing for you.

We're making you this offer to introduce you to the benefits of the Reader Service™– FREE home delivery of brand-new Temptation novels, at least a month before they are available in the shops, FREE gifts and a monthly Newsletter packed with information, competitions, author profiles and lots more...

Accepting these FREE books and gift places you under no obligation to buy, you may cancel at any time, even after receiving just your free shipment. Simply complete the coupon below and send it to:

MILLS & BOON READER SERVICE, FREEPOST, CROYDON, SURREY, CR9 3WZ.

READERS IN EIRE PLEASE SEND COUPON TO PO BOX 4546, DUBLIN 24

NO STAMP NEEDED

Yes, please send me 4 free Temptation novels and a mystery gift. I understand that unless you hear from me, I will receive 4 superb new titles every month for just £2.20* each, postage and packing free. I am under no obligation to purchase any books and I may cancel or suspend my subscription at any time, but the free books and gift will be mine to keep in any case.
(I am over 18 years of age)

T7YE

Ms/Mrs/Miss/Mr_____

BLOCK CAPS PLEASE

Address_____

_____

_____ Postcode _____

Barbara

DELINSKY

THROUGH MY EYES

A Friend in Need...
is a whole lot of trouble!

Jill Moncrief had to face painful memories to
help a friend in trouble. Hot-shot attorney Peter
Hathaway was just the man she needed—but
the last man on earth she should want...